"So, you'll do it, then?" Melanie Carlisle nodded as if they'd just agreed on something.

Cap pressed the heel of his free hand against his ear, muffling the irritating roar in his head. Had he missed a crucial part of the conversation? He squinted. "I'm sorry?"

"I'm new in town and I need someone to tear down my white picket fence," she said, as if it were the most normal thing in the world.

"Oh. Well." Cap looked around, again expecting to find a handyman standing right behind him. When one didn't materialize, he offered the sledgehammer back to Melanie. "Good luck with that, and welcome to Lovestruck."

Melanie didn't so much as flinch. Nor did she take the tool from him. "It would be really great if you could do it."

"Me," he said flatly. "But why?"

"Because I can't, obviously. Don't get me wrong— I totally would, but..." She waved a graceful hand in the vicinity of her midsection.

She raised her brows at him, and he reluctantly took a closer look at her stomach. There, beneath the gathered pleats of her breezy gingham dress, he spotted the unmistakable outline of a small baby bump. Something inside him softened.

"Right, of course you can't," he heard himself say.

"It's all settled then. You'll do it. Right now would be great—perfect, actually." She beamed at him.

A man could lose himself in a smile like that.

LOVESTRUCK, VERMONT
Find

D0950311

Dear Reader,

Welcome back to Lovestruck! *The Trouble with Picket Fences* is the third book in my Lovestruck, Vermont series for Harlequin Special Edition.

The first two Lovestruck books feature firemen who work at Engine Co. 24 on Main Street. In this new story, I decided to write about the patriarch of the firehouse, Cap McBride. Cap has been a father figure and role model for the other firefighters in Lovestruck for years. He's a single dad to a teenage son, a lifelong resident of Lovestruck and his service to the fire department means everything to him. In the opening of this book, he's reeling from a medical diagnosis that might end his career. Then along comes a quirky ex–Miss America who turns what's left of his world upside down.

Former beauty queen Melanie Carlisle is new to Vermont, new to Lovestruck and very, very new to small-town life. She's also still coming to terms with her decision to start a family all on her own at the age of forty. She just has one rule for her new life—no white picket fences. In fact, she's so averse to the offensive structure that when she meets Cap in the hammer aisle of the local hardware store, she convinces him to take hers apart.

I especially loved writing this story because even though Cap and Melanie are a bit older than the other characters in the Lovestruck series, their love story teaches them that it's never too late to start a dazzling new adventure.

I hope you enjoy this springtime trip to Vermont. As always, thank you so much for reading. And please look for the next book in the Lovestruck series, coming this Christmas.

Happy reading!

Teri Wilson

The Trouble with Picket Fences

TERI WILSON

HARLEQUIN

SPECIAL EDITION

HARLEQUIN®
SPECIAL EDITION™

Recycling programs for this product may not exist in your area.

ISBN-13: 978-1-335-40480-0

The Trouble with Picket Fences

Copyright © 2021 by Teri Wilson

Teri Wilson is a *Publishers Weekly* bestselling author of romance and romantic comedy. Several of Teri's books have been adapted into Hallmark Channel Original Movies, most notably *Unleashing Mr. Darcy*. She is also a recipient of the prestigious RITA® Award for excellence in romance fiction for her novel *The Bachelor's Baby Surprise*. Teri has a major weakness for cute animals and pretty dresses, and she loves following the British royal family. Visit her at www.teriwilson.net.

For the first responders and medical workers who give of themselves to keep others safe.

Chapter One

If Melanie Carlisle was good at one thing, it was taking bad lemons and turning them into lemonade. Truth be told, she was rather famous for it.

As in, national-television-and-a-book-deal famous. There may have also been a tiara involved, but that part had come later. Still, the rhinestone sparkler held a place of honor in a special, custom-made, Lucite box on a plush velvet cushion. Back in Dallas, Melanie had kept the box smack in the middle of a trophy case, along with the rest of her sashes and crowns. Her students often stood with their noses pressed against the glass, gazing at all the dazzle and glitz. Every now and then, she'd remove the crown from the box and let them take turns trying it on.

But Melanie wasn't in Dallas anymore. As of two hours ago, she'd become the newest resident of Lovestruck, Vermont—a tiny, picturesque town dotted with covered bridges, red barns and fields of bright yellow daffodils as sunny and cheery as, well, a pitcher of fresh-squeezed lemonade. Because Melanie was once again doing what she did best—taking her bad lemons and making them into something deliciously wonderful. A fresh, new start.

Except things hadn't started off quite as deliciously she'd hoped.

"This can't be it," she said to her real-estate agent as she stood staring at the darling two-bedroom cottage that she'd chosen from the Realtor's website.

The house looked just as pretty as it had online, with pink clapboard siding and swirly Victorian gingerbread trim. It had a cute octagon-shaped tower attached to its right side that looked like an actual turret. Melanie had fallen head over heels for the sweet little bungalow the instant she'd seen it.

It was the sort of house where kids might run

across the lawn and play in the sprinkler during the summertime, where neighbors would pop over to borrow a cup of sugar and where red, white and blue bunting might hang from the front porch railing on the Fourth of July. Melanie pictured bicycle parades and block parties, barbecue cookouts and mommy-and-me play groups, trick-or-treating on Halloween and Easter egg hunts in spring. Old-fashioned lemonade stands—obviously—with handmade signs scrawled in crayon.

Best of all, despite the cottage's obvious charm, it was missing the one thing that Melanie refused to abide…or so she'd thought.

"Where did that white picket fence come from?" She waved a hand at the offending barrier. "This wasn't in the online photos."

No white picket fences.

It had been Melanie's only caveat.

"Um." Charity Reed, junior agent at Lovestruck Realty, glanced at the fence, a tiny crinkle forming in her smooth forehead. Melanie hoped Charity Reed knew enough to appreciate her skin's natural elasticity. Melanie sure hadn't at that age. Live and learn. "It's been there for a month or so. I think the homeowner added it once the house had been on the market for a while. The fence is so new that we hadn't had a chance to update the online listing before you made the offer on the property."

This was what Melanie got for buying a house over the internet. She supposed it could have been worse. At least the cottage seemed to be in decent shape, white picket eyesore notwithstanding.

"Such fences are quite common here in Lovestruck," Charity said. "Nearly all of the homes in the town's historic district have them."

"I'm aware," Melanie said, flashing her beauty-queen smile.

Eliminating the cottages with quaint little fences had reduced Melanie's online list of potential homes by about 90 percent. In the end, she'd been left with a choice between the charming pink Victorian or a repurposed red barn on the edge of town. Melanie wasn't exactly a barn sort of girl.

Then again, she'd never been the mommy sort, either. But that was about to change—just five more months to go.

She took a deep breath and rested a protective hand on her small baby bump. What in the world would her old pageant coach say if she could see Melanie now? Pregnant at forty, starting a brand-new business in a brand-new town.

Alone.

Not exactly where she'd thought she'd end up when she'd been crowned Miss America at the tender age of twenty. But tiaras and low-level fame aside, nothing in Melanie's life had been anywhere close to being perfect or predictable, including the manner in which she'd taken on the mantle of Miss America. She was used to it by now.

Lemons to lemonade.

"I'd like to have the fence removed," she said.

The Realtor blinked. "Removed?"

"Yes." Melanie nodded. "The sooner, the better."

Charity bit her lip. "Are you sure? It's brand-new, really lovely and adds quite a bit to the home's character and property value."

"I'm absolutely sure." A wave of queasy exhaustion washed over Melanie. She needed to get her feet up for a bit, but she also needed to walk around the corner to Main Street and check on her new children's boutique. And the pink cottage was presumably filled with boxes that needed to be unpacked, plus all the other items she'd sent ahead of her arrival. She didn't have time for morning sickness—at least not until she'd dealt with the most important thing on her agenda.

She cast a meaningful look at the fence and then back toward her real-estate agent.

"I'm sure it won't be too much of a hassle to remove if that's what you want," Charity said.

Melanie wanted it, most definitely. Alas, she had little to no experience with tearing down aesthetically pleasing wooden structures. "Great. How do we go about doing that?"

Charity's eyes lit up at Melanie's unfortunate use of a plural collective pronoun.

"We?" Her gaze drifted to Melanie's hand, still placed atop her rapidly growing midsection. Charity beamed. "Perhaps your husband could take it down?"

Melanie should have seen that one coming. Her beauty-queen smile grew strained around the edges. "I'm not married."

"Oh, I'm sorry." Charity pressed a hand to her chest. "Bless your heart."

Melanie ground her teeth. Her heart had been blessed enough to last a lifetime back in Dallas, thank you very much. No matter what it might look like on the outside, Melanie had her life completely under control. She didn't want or need anyone's sympathy. All she needed was a hammer. Or, better yet, a handyman.

"No need to apologize. I'm fine—*we're* fine," she said, because she was part of a family now, after all. And that family was *everything* to Melanie. She'd upended her entire life for her unborn baby girl, and she'd do it again in a heartbeat.

That was one of the benefits of what her doctor back in Texas had annoyingly referred to as a *geriatric pregnancy.* While the vocabulary of her condition might be slightly insulting, she was old enough to appreciate the miraculous nature of what was happening. She'd waited a long time to be a mother, and she intended to cherish every moment of her pregnancy.

Which was exactly why the fence had to go.

"Of course. I understand." Charity nodded in a way that told Melanie she didn't understand at all, but that was fine, too. If beauty queens were good at one thing, it was rising above common misconceptions about who they were and what they stood for.

Charity Reed would learn that lesson soon enough, as would the rest of Melanie's new hometown. She had big plans—for herself, her baby and the entire community of Lovestruck.

First things first, though. "Now about that fence."

Lovestruck Fire Department Captain Jason McBride lingered in the tool aisle of the mom-

and-pop hardware store on Main Street, staring blankly ahead at the hammer display.

Why had he come in here on the way back to the station from his doctor's appointment, again?

He pressed hard on his temples in an effort to force his careening thoughts back on track. There'd been a reason for this errand. He was certain of it. He just couldn't remember what it was.

Calm down. It wasn't the worst *news. You're not dying or anything. Everything's going to be fine.*

He squeezed his eyes closed and tried not to think about the look of concern on Dr. Martin's face or the intimidating words printed at the top of the brochure the doctor had handed him. NIHL—Noise-Induced Hearing Loss Accompanied by Tinnitus.

It wasn't a brain tumor, as he'd feared. That was the good news, and Jason was grateful for it. He truly was.

But the bad news was indeed bad. NIHL was permanent, as was the tinnitus. How was he supposed to live—and, more importantly, do his job—with a constant roar in his ears? Just yesterday, he'd missed an entire conversation over his headset. Luckily, it was nothing dire. But what would happen next time?

Make no mistake, there would definitely be a next time. Jason occupied the top spot in the LFD. His career was so integral to his life that he didn't even go by his own name anymore. His men called him Cap, short for Captain. It had been his nickname for so long that everyone in town called him Cap.

Cap's own son had thought it was his actual name until he'd gotten old enough to read the label on his subscription to *Firehouse* magazine. "Who's Jason McBride?" he'd asked, wide-eyed in a pair of footie pajamas decorated with tiny fire trucks and Dalmatian puppies.

Cap had just laughed. "That's me, bud. Your daddy."

He didn't feel like a Jason anymore, though. He hadn't in a long, long time. The fire department was in his blood, as much a part of him as his limbs, his lungs…his heart. He liked being Cap. He liked giving back to the community he loved in such a real and tangible way, and he cared about the younger firefighters in the department as if they were his own. If the LFD was a family, then Cap was their patriarch.

He wasn't ready to give that up. He couldn't even fathom it.

"Caulk," he said to the rows of hammers.

That's what Cap was supposed to be buying—caulk for the firehouse showers.

The hammers uttered nothing in response. Still, it took Cap another full minute to stop staring into space and get moving. He really needed to get his head in the game. He'd have plenty of time to worry about the brochure in his pocket later—after his shift, or tomorrow after Eli's junior varsity lacrosse game, post-game pizza and the ongoing misery of Eli's calculus homework.

Meanwhile, caulk.

Cap turned toward the sealants aisle, but just as he rounded the corner, a woman with waves of tumbling strawberry blond hair and striking green eyes pointed a sledgehammer at him.

"You," she said.

Cap glanced around, certain she was talking to somebody else, but they were the only two shoppers in the aisle. "Me?"

"Yes, you." She thrust the sledgehammer toward his chest. "You look like you know how to use one of these."

For reasons he couldn't being to contemplate, Cap obediently took hold of the sledgehammer. "I do, yes. But…"

But who the heck are you and why are you shoving tools at me?

He looked more closely at her emerald eyes, the graceful curve of her neck, the jaunty little tilt of her chin. There was something vaguely familiar about the hammer-wielding woman, but Cap couldn't seem to place her.

Then again, he'd been going out on emergency calls in rural Vermont for more than two decades. Cap met a lot of a people. Something told him he would have remembered her, though.

"I'm sorry," he said. "Have we met?"

"Melanie Carlisle. It's a pleasure to meet you." She stuck her hand out.

No wedding ring. Cap fumbled with the sledgehammer and nearly dropped it in an attempt to shake Melanie Carlisle's delicate hand. "Cap McBride."

He could feel sweat breaking out on the back of his neck. Cap wasn't accustomed to making small talk with beautiful women in the hardware store. Once upon a time, maybe, but that had been a while ago. He hadn't even been on a date in almost a decade.

People didn't date anymore, though, did they? That's what Eli told him. They hung out. They hooked up. They Netflixed and chilled. Cap hadn't done many of those things, either. But he was fairly certain none of those activities began at the intersection of the hammer and adhesive aisles.

"So, you'll do it, then?" Melanie Carlisle nodded as if they'd just agreed on something.

Cap pressed the heel of his free hand against his ear, muffling the irritating roar in his head. Had he missed a crucial part of the conversation?

He squinted. "I'm sorry?"

"I'm new in town and I need someone to tear down my white picket fence," she said as if it were the most normal thing in the world.

"Oh. Well." Cap looked around, again expecting to find a handyman standing right behind him. When one didn't materialize, he offered the sledgehammer back to Melanie. "Good luck with that, and welcome to Lovestruck."

Why in the world would someone want to tear down a picket fence? They were all the rage in Lovestruck. Cap was pretty sure the mayor was on a not-so-secret mission to get one in every yard in the historic district.

Melanie didn't so much as flinch. Nor did she take the tool from him. "It would be really great if you could do it."

"Me," he said flatly. "But why?"

Why, indeed. Why was he still sticking around for this bizarre conversation? He should just put down the hammer, grab his caulk and go. He had work to do, a teenage son to contend with—all on his own, thank you very much—and a potentially career-ending medical diagnosis to absorb. Cap had no intention of making firewood out of this strange woman's white picket fence. Zero.

"Because I can't, obviously. Don't get me wrong—I totally would, but…" She waved a graceful hand in the vicinity of her midsection.

Was this a trick? Cap knew he was old-fashioned. Eli and the guys at the fire station never failed to mock his fondness for dad jokes, even though Cap thought they were just jokes, period. Cap also liked to look women in the eye as a matter of basic respect and decency. But Melanie seemed to be guiding his attention elsewhere.

She raised her eyebrows at him, and he reluctantly took a closer look at her stomach. There, beneath the gathered pleats of her breezy gingham dress, he spotted the unmistakable outline of a small baby bump. Something inside of him softened.

"Right, of course, you can't," he heard himself say.

"It's all settled then. You'll do it. Right now

would be great—perfect, actually." She beamed at him, and for a second, Cap forgot all about his doctor's appointment, the caulk at the firehouse and Eli's failing math grade.

Pregnant women glowed. That's what everyone always said, anyway. This felt different, though. Melanie Carlisle's smile seemed to burrow into Cap's chest and make itself at home there.

A man could lose himself in a smile like that.

Not him, obviously—a different man. A younger man. A man who didn't feel like he was on the verge of losing everything he held dear.

Day by day, brick by brick, Cap had been building a wall around himself. He'd been doing it for months, without telling a soul about the symptoms he'd been dealing with. Today he'd finally begun to face the truth, and now fate had tossed a beautiful woman in his path. His walls were going up, and for some crazy reason, Melanie Carlisle wanted Cap to tear hers down to the ground.

The irony of it was unmistakably bittersweet, and just too damn tempting to resist.

He rested the sledgehammer on his shoulder. The caulk could wait. "Lead the way."

Chapter Two

Melanie stood at her kitchen counter, stirring a pitcher of fresh-squeezed lemonade with her favorite wooden spoon while she gazed out the window and watched the man she'd met at the hardware store systematically disassemble her white picket fence. She didn't normally coerce strange men into doing her favors like this. Melanie was more of a do-it-herself kind of girl. But desperate times called for desperate measures and all that. As much as she didn't want to think of herself as geriatric—ugh, why couldn't she forget about that mortifying word?—she was well aware that any pregnancy after forty was considered high-risk. She couldn't go around wielding sledgehammers anymore.

Not that she'd had much occasion to do so in the past, but still.

The muscles in Cap's broad shoulders flexed beneath his LFD T-shirt as he added another white board to the pile of discarded lumber in her front yard. Melanie wondered if he was a firefighter. Probably so, given his attire and also given his proficiency at manual labor. He was making quick work of the fence. She could definitely picture him chopping away at a smoldering pile of rubble with an ax or carrying a baby away from a burning building.

Melanie blinked. Hard. She didn't *want* this man darting around her imagination, no matter how heroic he seemed. And she was really getting tired of the annoying habit she'd developed of trying to picture every man she met interacting with a child. She blamed it on Greg. Once a man told you that he had absolutely zero interest in having children—*ever*—it was hard not to wonder if other men felt the same. How had she failed to realize that in the eleven years she and Greg had dated, she'd never seen him hold a baby? Not once. It seemed statistically impossible, but alas, it was true. In the wake of their breakup, Melanie had done a thorough inventory of both her memories and her photo albums. Across the board, Greg's arms remained notably baby-free.

Now, whenever she set eyes on a man, Melanie couldn't help but wonder about his infant-holding history. She refused to get caught off guard again, although she wasn't sure why. It wasn't as if she were looking for a husband. Or even a boyfriend—been there, done that, got the T-shirt. She had a new baby to think about. A new business. A new home. Her plate was beyond full as it was.

Even so, she would have bet money on the fact that Cap had held his fair share of babies. Probably his share plus Greg's neglected share combined, a fact that didn't sway Melanie in the slightest. She liked to think of her baby-holding scale as an odd science experiment of sorts, not a measure of attractiveness. But the man had agreed to do her a massive favor without knowing anything about her other than her name, so the least she could do was whip him up a pitcher of lemonade.

It *was* her specialty, after all. And being America's unofficial lemonade queen, she'd carefully labeled her kitchen boxes to ensure that her juicer, wooden spoon and glass pitcher were readily accessible.

Although, her reign as America's lemonade queen was surely over by now. It had been years since she'd been in the public eye. More than a decade. The only people who remembered her quirky lemonade routine were those on the pageant circuit, and she wouldn't be seeing them anymore now that she'd closed up shop on her coaching business.

Which was fine. A fresh start was exactly what she wanted. Melanie just sort of hoped it came with a few new friends, because she was used to being surrounded by a gaggle of teenage girls. Dallas had been rhinestones, evening gowns and road trips with her students every weekend to tiny local pageants held in community centers and high-school gymnasiums. She'd been in Vermont less than a day, but so far, it had mostly been quiet. So quiet that the little voice in the back of her head was the only one she'd had much interaction with, and unfortunately, that voice had an annoyingly anxious edge.

You don't know a soul here. What happens if something goes wrong with the pregnancy?

Who's going to run the boutique if you get stuck on bed rest?

Her hands shook as she poured Cap's lemonade into a tall, slender glass.

Women your age have a forty percent chance of miscarrying.

The glass overflowed, spilling sticky liquid onto the counter of her new kitchen. Melanie's face went hot as dabbed at it with one of her cherry-print dish towels.

She willed her hands to stop shaking as she carried the lemonade outside, and as soon as she caught an up close glimpse of Cap's strong back and the muscles in his forearms as he tore another plank from the fence, the worrisome voice in the back of her head quieted down. That sledgehammer looked sort of fun. Cathartic, even. Maybe she'd give a try…

In another five months or so.

"Hi. I thought you could use a nice, cold drink," she said to the huge LFD splashed across the back of his navy T-shirt.

He kept hacking away at the fence without so much as a pause. Perhaps Melanie wasn't the only one who needed a little catharsis.

She repeated herself and then continued to watch for a minute, waiting for him to turn around. When he didn't, she tiptoed around him, giving his swinging arm a wide berth.

The sledgehammer whizzed past her and froze with a hitch, in midair, as Cap stumbled backward.

"Oh, wow. Are you okay? I didn't see you." The color drained from his chiseled face as he looked her up and down. "Or, um, hear you."

"I'm totally fine. You missed me by a mile." Well, maybe not a mile. But a good foot or so. "You seemed very…focused."

His stern mouth curved into a frown.

"Focused," he echoed.

"Very." Melanie nodded. "I'm sure that's why you didn't hear me."

"You're probably right," he said, and then he looked away, focusing on what was left of the white picket fence instead of Melanie.

This whole interaction was beginning to feel awkward and weird, but what else could she expect given the fact that she'd dragged a man out of the hardware store pretty much against his will?

Melanie pasted a Miss Congeniality–worthy smile on her face and offered him the glass. "I made you some lemonade."

"Thank you, but—" He waved a hand in that

way people did when they were about to politely decline something, but then his brow furrowed as he spotted a paper-thin lemon slice perched on the rim of the glass. He pointed at the lemonade. "Is that homemade?"

Melanie nodded. "Fresh-squeezed, thanks to my new lemon tree out back."

What were the odds? Melanie had never had her own lemon tree before, and she hadn't realized the spindly tree planted in the big barrel on her back porch produced Meyer lemons until she'd arrived in Vermont in person and seen the shiny yellow fruit hanging from its branches. It felt like a sign—a sign that everything would indeed be just fine. A sign that she'd done the right thing. A sign that she belonged here in Lovestruck.

"In that case, how can I refuse?" Cap took the glass from her and drank a big sip of lemonade. When he swallowed, muscles flexed in his neck and reminded Melanie of the old Diet Coke commercials featuring hunky guys gulping down soda in a jaw-droppingly sexy manner.

Weird, she hadn't thought about those silly commercials in years.

"This is fantastic," Cap said, peering into his glass. He looked up and met Melanie's gaze, eyes narrowing. "Wait a minute. You're *her*, aren't you? The lemonade queen."

Melanie felt her cheeks go warm. Maybe her reign wasn't quite over, after all. "You certainly have a good memory. That was a million years ago."

His smile turned sheepish. "From what I remember, you made quite an impression."

A delightful thrill skittered through Melanie. Was he talking about the impression she'd made on *him* or the country at large?

She cleared her throat. He meant the latter, obviously. She'd been on all the morning talk shows the day after the pageant, famously becoming the best-known runner-up in Miss America history. What had the host of that big network television show called her? *Most famous loser.* So very flattering. It sounded almost as bad as *geriatric pregnancy.*

"Right. Well." Melanie crossed her arms and promptly uncrossed them. Where was her trademark beauty-queen grace? She suddenly felt like she didn't know what to do with herself without a glass of lemonade in her hands. "I'm still surprised you recognized me. Most people who remember the pageant think I look familiar but can't seem to place me."

The fact that he could indeed place her shouldn't have made her feel so sparkly inside, but it did—nearly as light and glittery as her Miss America crown. Sometimes her pageants days seemed so far away that they felt like a dream instead of reality, especially lately. It was nice to feel seen…and not just because she was sporting a baby bump and an empty ring finger.

"Thanks again for this," she said, waving a hand at what was left of the fence. "I really appreciate it."

"No problem," Cap said. "You caught me at a good time. I wasn't all that eager to get back to the firehouse."

Melanie opened her mouth to ask why, but before she could get the words out, a cell phone started ringing—his, obviously. She could see the outline of it in the pocket of his cargo pants, and she'd left her own phone back on the kitchen counter.

He didn't make a move to answer it. He just stood there as if waiting for her to continue their conversation.

"Do you need to get that?" she said. He was supposed to be at work right now, apparently. What if it was something important, like a fire or a kitten stuck in a tree somewhere? Lovestruck seemed like just the sort of place where the rescue of a fluffy kitten would be considered a dire situation.

Cap's eyebrows drew together. "Get what?"

Wow. Melanie had never met someone who could tune out the ringing of a cell phone, herself included. She envied his ability to live in the moment.

Her gaze flitted toward the pocket of his cargo pants, and then back toward his face. His handsome, handsome face. He'd somehow gotten more attractive since their initial meeting in the hammer aisle. Was this what all the parenting books meant when they talked about pregnancy hormones?

"Your, um, phone is ringing," she said.

"Oh." His face fell. For a second, Melanie almost thought she saw a flicker of panic in his warm brown eyes. "My phone. Yeah, I should probably get it. Sorry."

"It's okay, really. I'm totally monopolizing your time." She held out a hand for his empty glass. "I'll take that and give you some privacy."

"Thanks." He handed her the tumbler. "And thanks for the lemonade. It was delicious."

"Anytime." Melanie smiled, but her fireman-turned-handyman was already looking down, fishing his phone from his pocket.

There was no reason whatsoever for her to feel disappointed. She didn't even know the man, and again, a kitten could be in jeopardy somewhere.

But as she clutched the glass to her chest and walked across her lovely new lawn in her lovely new town, she couldn't help feeling just a little bit lonely. Being the new girl in town might be harder than she'd thought it would be.

Cap's heart hammered as fast as a jackrabbit's as he scrambled to answer his phone. He hadn't even heard the blasted thing ringing, just like he hadn't heard Melanie sneaking up behind a few minutes ago.

Sneaking...really? She's a beauty queen, not a ninja.

It wasn't her fault. She was just being nice, offering him some of her famous Miss America lemonade. But she could have gotten hurt, damn it. She was *pregnant*, and he could have knocked her silly with the ridiculously heavy sledgehammer she'd forced into his hands at the hardware store.

And whose fault would that *have been?*

Cap's jaw clenched. He would have been to blame, obviously.

What was he going to do? He couldn't escape what was happening to him. Ripping apart Melanie's fence for the past hour had actually felt good. For a while there, he'd felt like his old self again. Competent. *Needed*.

And then the roaring in his ears had nearly caused him to clobber a pregnant woman. He hadn't even heard his own phone ringing.

"Hello?" he said into his device, trying his best to tamp down the rising panic in his gut.

"Is this Captain McBride?"

"Yes," he said, squinting toward Melanie Carlisle's little pink house. The cottage suited her. It was pretty in a graceful, classic sort of way. Just like the former Miss America and her lemonade.

"This is Principal Davis from Lovestruck High School. I'm afraid there's a situation with Eli. Do you have time to come in and chat for a bit?"

Cap's head began to throb in a way that had nothing to do with his constant tinnitus. "Is Eli okay?"

"Yes. I'm so sorry. I should have led with that," the principal said. "Eli is fine. He's sitting right here in my office, as a matter of fact."

Cap nodded. Lovestruck was a small town, as idyllic as they came. Even so, he'd seen enough tragedy during his tenure as a first responder to know that so long as his son was safe, everything would be okay. He allowed himself to relax just a fraction. Whatever was going on, they'd deal with it.

"I'll be right there," he said.

Cap shoved the phone back into his pocket and organized the discarded pieces of Melanie's fence into a nice, neat pile before making his way up the steps of her front porch and knocking on the door. While he waited for her to answer, he noticed that the white pergola in her side yard could use a new coat of paint. Likewise, the spigot on her garden hose needed to be replaced. He wondered if Melanie had someone who could help her with those chores.

Of course not. If she did, he wouldn't be standing there with sweat pouring down his back after ripping her fence to shreds.

The door swung open, and she smiled at him. Cap knew it was a cliché to say that pregnant women glowed, but Melanie did. He'd have had to be blind not to notice the slight flush to her peaches-and-cream complexion or the way her strawberry blond hair fell around her shoulders in full, bouncy waves. She was a literal beauty queen, so obviously she was attractive. But there was a loveliness about her that Cap couldn't quite put his finger on, like trying to hold sunlight in his hands.

"Hi." She held the door open wider. "Would you like to come in?"

Cap shook his head. "No, I actually need to get going."

He resisted the urge to explain about the call from Eli's principal. No good could come from talking about his personal problems. If Cap cracked open the seal on everything he'd been dealing with in the last few months, all of it might come tumbling out and the last thing he wanted was to spill his guts to a total stranger.

"Oh." Her pretty, heart-shaped mouth tipped into a frown.

Cap had the nonsensical impulse to tell her one of his dad jokes, just to make her smile again.

Then she looked past him, toward the stack of wooden planks in her yard. She was worried about the fence, because of course she was.

It's not your problem, he reminded himself. Cap didn't owe this woman a thing. He'd already gone above and beyond what any sane person would have done after meeting her in the hardware store, and she'd still yet to explain her hatred for the fence in question.

Just walk away. You have your own problems to deal with.

"I can come back tomorrow," he offered. "If that works for you?"

Tomorrow was his day off. He had laundry to do and meals to plan, not to mention a pretty sizable list of things that needed to be fixed at his own house. Eli had a lacrosse game in the afternoon, and afterward, they always joined the rest of the team for pizza. All of that left zero time for being a former Miss America's manservant.

But Melanie's smile returned, and the tightness that had wound its way around Cap's heart at the doctor's office eased somewhat…just enough for him to breathe again.

"That would be wonderful," she said.

He nodded. "See you tomorrow."

"It's a date."

Chapter Three

It's so not a date.

Melanie had wanted to reel the words back into her mouth the moment she'd said them, but there hadn't been time. Cap had just looked at her a little strangely and taken off, descending her porch steps with purpose. And why wouldn't he? He clearly had other things to do besides help a pregnant damsel in distress.

Well, she might be carrying a baby, but Melanie was no damsel in distress. Today was a new day. She'd spent the first evening in her new cottage unpacking boxes and when she'd woken up this morning, the little pink house had almost felt like home. Now she just needed to bring that same nesting energy to her new boutique on Main Street.

She also needed to stop thinking about Cap and their awkward goodbye the day before—a feat that would have been much more easily accomplished had Lovestruck Engine Company 24 not been located directly across the street from her shop. Melanie snuck a glance toward the redbrick building with the shiny red fire truck parked out front, but her knight in cargo pants was nowhere to be seen. That was probably for the best. She didn't have time for distractions this morning—particularly the sort of distractions that reminded her of Patrick Dempsey on an exceedingly good hair day.

Melanie refocused her attention on the rack of tiny clothes in front of her. Toddler outfits in colorful dinosaur prints were lined up, from big to small. She spaced the hangers evenly apart and eyed the display of plastic dinosaurs that she'd arranged atop the rack to make sure everything was just so. The shop was scheduled to open in less than a minute, and her T. rex kept falling over. Melanie never had these sorts of problems when she was a pageant coach.

Just as she was getting her mini Jurassic Park situated, the bells on the boutique door rang, announcing someone's arrival. Melanie turned, half expecting to see Cap McBride walking through the door. Instead, she found two women in yoga clothes holding paper coffee cups that had fragrant steam coming from the tiny holes in their plastic lids.

"Good morning." One of the women waved with her free hand. "I'm Felicity Ericson, and this is Madison Cole. We came to welcome you to Lovestruck."

"You're new here, right? Word on the street is that you just bought the boutique. And the cute pink house just a few blocks over?" Madison tipped her head in the direction of Melanie's cottage.

"Good gravy, Madison." Felicity rolled her eyes. "You're going to scare her to death. She might not be used to how…*intimate* small towns can be."

Melanie glanced back and forth between the two women. Felicity was right. In her wildest dreams, Melanie hadn't expected two complete strangers to already know this much about her. But the women seemed harmless enough, and it wasn't as if Melanie had never been the topic of conversation before.

"Sorry." Madison winced. "I'm actually from New York, originally. I should probably know to turn down the small-town charm a notch or two. We're just really excited about someone new taking over the boutique."

Madison offered Melanie one of the paper cups. "We brought you a maple latte. Don't worry, it's decaf."

Decaf…because Melanie was pregnant and that little personal detail was also public knowledge already. The devil worked hard, but the Lovestruck rumor mill worked harder, apparently.

"Thanks." Melanie took the cup. She had no choice, because whatever a maple latte was, it smelled absolutely divine. "I'm Melanie, but something tells me you already know my name."

Felicity's cheeks went pink. Yep, they knew.

"I run the yoga studio a few doors down," she said. "And Madison writes a fashion column for the local paper, the *Lovestruck Bee*."

Melanie felt her eyes goes wide. "A fashion column? In rural Vermont?"

She'd just found her people. Technically, they'd found her, but either way, Melanie had a feeling the three of them were going to become fast friends.

"Hard to believe, but true. How it came about is kind of a long story, but slowly and surely I'm whipping this town into stylish shape." Madison glanced around the shop. "And so are you. Look at all these cute clothes!"

Melanie sipped her coffee while Felicity and Madison took in all the hard work that she'd been doing since seven this morning. She'd never tasted anything so delicious. The rich, sweet flavors of maple, caramel and vanilla didn't resemble the store-bought syrup she'd been eating all of her life in the slightest. She was beginning to understand why Vermonters felt so passionately about maple.

"Wait a minute." Felicity stopped in front of the cash register area where Melanie's Miss America crown was proudly displayed in its Lucite box. "Is this real?"

Melanie bit back a smile. Finally…a detail that the small-town rumor mill had missed. "Yes, it is."

Madison blinked, gaping at the crown. "You were Miss America?"

Melanie nodded. "A long time ago and only for ten days, but yes."

"Wait." Felicity's forehead scrunched. "How does someone become Miss America for only ten days?"

"I was kind of the underdog for the whole competition, but my talent program was really unique." Melanie shrugged. "The judges really liked it, and I ended up being the first runner-up—"

Madison snapped her fingers. "Oh! We did a throwback story on this at the magazine where I worked in New York. Almost a year later, the winner had to resign in disgrace and you took over her reign, right?"

"Yep." Melanie held up ten fingers. "For exactly ten days. I hold the world record for the shortest reign in Miss America history."

Madison grinned. "But it made you famous. You basically went viral."

Melanie laughed. "Back then, viral meant you stayed in bed with a box of tissues until it passed."

"You know what I mean." Madison turned to Felicity. "Melanie is one of the most famous Miss Americas ever."

"Are you still involved in pageants?" Felicity asked.

"I had a pageant-coaching business back in

Texas, but now I'm here. Starting over." Melanie found herself resting a hand on her baby bump. "People like the crown, though, so I thought I'd put it on display. I figured the kids might get a kick out it while their parents shopped."

"Would you think I was insane if I asked to try it on?" Felicity bit her bottom lip.

"Of course not," Melanie said, reaching into a drawer for the lock to the crown box. Honestly, if she had a penny for every time one of her students had begged to try on the crown, she'd be a millionaire by now.

She lifted the glittering tiara from its plush velvet pillow and placed it carefully on Felicity's head. Then she guided the woman by the shoulders until she stood in front of one of the boutique's Venetian-style mirrors, trimmed with sparkling etched glass—another new addition that Melanie had put in place early this morning. She had a thing for sparkle and glitz, a former occupational hazard.

"Oh, wow." Felicity let out a squeal. "Madison, take my picture. My phone is in my purse."

Felicity waved a hand toward a hot-pink handbag that looked like it was either a high-end Birkin bag or a very good imitation. Melanie tried not to stare at the unmistakable bite marks on the corner of the fancy purse. Someone had a very naughty dog, but she couldn't help admiring a woman who had a passion for both animals and high fashion.

"You two are making me feel like moving here might not have been the most impulsive, craziest thing I've ever done." Melanie swallowed.

Second-most impulsive, craziest thing, she reminded herself. The first had been visiting a sperm bank after her cringe-worthy breakup with Greg.

Madison laughed. "Trust me, whatever you're feeling right now, we've both been there. Give it time. Lovestruck is a special place. It can seem a bit overwhelming at first, and when you're new in town, it feels like everyone here has known each other for a century and you'll never fit in. But soon, you'll feel right at home."

Melanie hoped so—sooner, rather than later. Her baby would be born in five short months.

Madison snapped a few photos of Felicity, and as Felicity gingerly removed the crown from her head, Madison gasped. "Oh, my gosh, I have the best idea."

"Oh, no." Felicity winced and turned toward Melanie. "Madison once wrote an entire column on bedazzling diapers, so strap in. There's no telling where she's going with this."

"That column was tongue-in-cheek...sort of. Honestly, you bedazzle one diaper and you never hear the end of it." Madison waved a hand. "Anyway, I've got it—the perfect way for you to get to know everyone in town."

She beamed at Melanie.

Melanie tightened her grip on her maple latte. Did she even *want* to get to know everyone in town?

Yes. Yes, she did. That's what small-town life was all about, right? It was the very reason she'd moved to Lovestruck in the first place. She wanted her child to grow up in a place with summer bicycle parades, bake sales and old-fashioned Christmas festivals. Just because she was going to be a single mom didn't mean she had to be her baby's only support system. She wanted—*needed*—her child to grow up feeling loved, cherished and safe. Being part of something bigger than herself, part of a community like the one in Lovestruck, would mean just that.

"How?" Melanie asked. So far, her only real plan had been to launch the reopening of the boutique.

And to finish obliterating the white picket eyesore in her yard. Priorities, and all.

Madison's gaze darted to the crown and back toward Melanie. "A children's pageant!"

"What are we doing here?" Eli said as Cap pulled his truck into the driveway of Melanie Carlisle's little pink house.

The pile of white boards was right where Cap had left it the day before. Surrounded by only half of a picket fence, the cottage suddenly had a quirky, mysterious air about it—as if it knew a secret that no one else was privy to.

But perhaps Cap was just projecting. He'd be lying to himself if he'd said he wasn't curious about Melanie's pregnancy. There was no ring on her finger, and she'd given him no indication whatsoever that she had a man in her life. Even though it was clearly none of his business, he couldn't help wondering about the father of her baby—a fact that he chalked up to simple curiosity rather than any romantic interest in the single mother-to-be.

"I'm here to keep a promise," Cap said, shifting the truck into Park. "And you're here because you've been expelled from school for a day. Did you think I'd let you sleep in and play video games all day after you were caught cheating on your math test?"

"Calculus," Eli corrected under his breath.

Cap gritted his teeth. Calculus was math, wasn't it? Just a particularly excruciating variety of it. "Come on. That fence isn't going tear itself down."

He stepped out of the truck and reached into the back for the sledgehammer. Eli eyed it warily.

"I don't know how to use that," the boy said.

"Well, you're about to learn. You might even like it." Cap handed him the tool.

Eli took the hammer, clearly unprepared for the weight of its bulk. It looked as if his arm nearly jerked out right of its socket.

"Careful, it's heavy." Cap bit back a smile.

Yesterday had been a train wreck. Cap had thought things couldn't get worse after his doctor's appointment, but clearly, he'd thought wrong. Failing calculus was one thing, but cheating? That was another matter entirely.

Eli knew better. If his son hadn't appeared so guilt-stricken when Cap walked into the principal's office, he might have thought the entire episode had been some kind of mix-up. His kid didn't cheat. Except this time, he had.

"Dad, you know I only did it because I was

afraid of being benched, right?" Eli said as he hauled the sledgehammer onto his shoulder.

The lacrosse coach had strict rules when it came to the weekly games. If one of his players was failing a class, the kid got benched—a fate worse than death, as far as Eli was concerned.

"I know." Cap nodded. "But that still doesn't make it right. Plus now you've let your team down."

Eli looked at him, and for a second, he looked like a little boy again—wide-eyed and vulnerable. It had been a long time since Cap had seen such raw openness on his son's face. *Too* long.

Cap swallowed hard. "We'll get you a tutor, okay?"

"Okay." Eli nodded. "Thanks, Dad."

Cap's head ached. He wanted to blame it on the tinnitus, but he wasn't altogether sure that's what it was. He was just so tired of trying to hold everything together. On some level, this cheating business was his fault, wasn't it? What the heck did he know about integrals and derivatives? He should've gotten his kid a tutor a few months ago, right when Eli's math grade began to slip, instead of trying to figure things out on his own. Accepting help had never been Cap's strong suit, though. He liked being on the giving end of that equation, not the receiving one. It was just how he operated.

"So we're building a fence?" Eli said, shifting from one foot to the other.

"Tearing it down." Cap shrugged one shoulder and started marching across Melanie's green lawn.

Eli followed. "I don't get it. Why?"

That was the million-dollar question, wasn't it? Cap had no idea, but he'd lived in Lovestruck long enough to know that forcing a secret into the light of day was never a good thing. Melanie had her reasons, and if she'd felt like sharing them, she probably would have done so by now.

No matter. He was being neighborly, that's all. He would have done the same for anyone else in town that needed help.

"I have no idea," he said flatly. "Now get to work."

A children's pageant.

Melanie wasn't so sure at first, but the more she thought about it—and the more Madison and Felicity told her about the Lovestruck mommy crowd, who did things like enroll in baby-bootee-knitting classes and push their baby strollers to The Bean every morning en masse—the more she was convinced. Kid pageants had never really been her thing, especially the "glitz" events like the ones portrayed on tacky reality shows. But the simpler kind of pageants, the ones that emphasized community service and public speaking instead of hair spray and inappropriate costumes, were good for kids.

Pageants were a great way for children to develop good self-esteem and learn how to express themselves with poise and confidence. The general public had no idea how much emphasis the pageant system placed on volunteerism. The girls whom Melanie coached back in Texas read books to nursing home residents, walked shelter dogs, raised money for various community causes and tutored at-risk middle-school children. While other high-school kids were getting into trouble, her girls were learning what it meant to help people. Children were never too young to learn empathy and compassion.

Melanie just needed to figure out a way to tie the event to a worthy cause, and she'd be good to go. It would be fun, and maybe by the time it was all over, she'd be fully entrenched in the town—as much a part of Lovestruck as maple syrup. With any luck, Melanie might even have a group of moms she could turn to for help once the baby was born. A built-in support group.

Her new friend Madison just might be a genius.

After she and Felicity left, Melanie spent the rest of the day putting out her new merchandise. The inventory that had come with her purchase of the boutique was hopelessly dull and outdated. She wasn't sure she should even try to sell any of it. Who knew how long those items had sat on the shelves and rolling racks collecting dust? If her shop was going to attract customers, it needed a fresh, new start.

Of course, she couldn't help doing a little brainstorming about the pageant while she boxed things up and packed them away. A half hour after the boutique closed and she pulled up to her little pink house, she was still giddy with excitement over her plans. Then she spotted her pristine, picket-fence-free, emerald-green lawn and her heart gave a major tug.

Cap had come back, just like he'd said he would.

Perhaps Melanie shouldn't have been surprised that he'd kept his word. Anyone who performed such a favor for a random pregnant woman he didn't actually know had to be a stand-up guy. But she'd assumed he planned on coming back to finish the job after work. The last thing she'd expected was to come home and find a neatly stacked pile of repurposed firewood next to her front porch.

There it is, she thought as she eyed what was left of the fence. *My white picket dreams, all ready to go up in flames.*

It was a potent reminder of how she'd ended up in this tiny little town with her tiny little almost-family, all on her own. The next time she found herself gazing out the window of her boutique, hoping to catch a glimpse of Cap at the firehouse, she needed to march herself back to her cottage and take a good look at this sad little stack of lumber.

"It's just you and me now," she whispered to the swell of her abdomen, and an overwhelming weariness came over her.

Today had been a good day. She'd made some new friends, and after Madison and Felicity left, only three customers had inquired about Melanie's nonexistent husband after they'd noticed her baby bump. But pregnancy was exhausting.

The *G* word floated through her consciousness—*geriatric*—and for the first time, it almost felt applicable.

Wherever Cap McBride was, she doubted his

evening plans involved a grilled cheese sandwich and bowl of tomato soup while soaking his aching feet in an Epsom-salt bath—yet another reason she needed to forget about the hammer-wielding fireman.

Easier said than done.

Chapter Four

Cap dropped off Eli at school bright and early the following morning, then sat in the car and watched as his son entered the building with his lacrosse stick slung over his shoulder.

He couldn't quite bring himself to be happy about his fourteen-year-old's one-day suspension, but it had meant a rare chance to spend a full day together since it coincided with Cap's day off from the station. They'd spent hours at Melanie Carlisle's house, finishing off the fence and then moving on to other minor chores that needed to be done to the property's exterior.

All the while, Cap told himself he wasn't dragging his feet, waiting for the erstwhile beauty queen to come home. He was enjoying himself, that's all. And he knew that once Eli walked back through the door at home, he'd have better things to do than hang out with his dear old dad. Namely, his calculus homework.

Today, things were back to normal. At least Cap hoped so. No more tearing down fences, no more angry calls from the school principal, no more accidentally signing up to be at the beck and call of his new neighbor, no matter how lovely she seemed. Cap had his own problems to contend with. He did his best to push them to the back of his mind as he strode into the firehouse.

"Morning, Cap." Jack Cole, Engine Company 24's second-in-command, waved a spatula in greeting as Cap entered the building.

Jack was the station's official lieutenant and unofficial chef. Before Madison Jules had swept into town in her fancy designer clothes and stolen Jack's heart, he'd been a single dad to twin baby girls. Cooking had been the only thing that seemed to help with his constant exhaustion, and even now that he was happily married and Madison Jules officially went by Madison Cole, the habit had stuck. Much to the delight of his fellow firefighters, Cap included.

"Morning." Cap plucked a muffin from a platter in the middle of the kitchen counter and took a bite. The taste of warm, sweet blueberries filled his senses, along with a hint of something else. Something that nearly made him moan out loud.

"These are fantastic." Cap inspected the half-eaten muffin. "What's different about them?"

Jack shrugged. "I added some freshly grated lemon rind."

Lemon. Visions of Melanie Carlisle and her Miss America smile flitted through Cap's consciousness.

He put down the muffin. "Interesting."

Jack regarded him through narrowed eyes until Wade Ericson, one of the other members of the C shift, breezed into the firehouse.

"Morning, all," Wade said, glancing from Jack to Cap and back again. "Have you told him?"

Cap frowned. "Told me what?"

Jack and Wade were the most promising firefighters in the department. Sure, Cap occasionally had to step in and offer some fatherly advice to the two younger men, like the time Jack had decided that writing snarky, anonymous letters to the editor of the local paper was a good idea. Or last Christmas, when Wade suddenly wanted to adopt a baby that had been abandoned at the firehouse under Vermont's safe-haven law. But as far as Cap was concerned, being a mentor to the younger men was part of his job. Someday, Cap would be gone and Jack or Wade would be the one in charge. They'd do the same for the newer recruits. That's how the LFD worked, and Cap wouldn't have it any other way.

He just hoped that *someday* managed to stay as far away as possible. Cap wasn't ready to give up this place. He didn't know what to do without the fire department. Ten years ago, when his wife, Lucy, had died, this job had saved Cap. Fighting a fire was all-consuming. It demanded everything from a person. When Cap was battling a blaze, there wasn't room in his head— or heart—for anything else. For those heated, heightened moments, he was free. Free from the mistakes of his past. Free from worries about the future. There was only the present, and the feeling that if he tried hard enough and did everything right, he could exert some control over whatever came next. He could make it right in the end.

Cap's ears roared. Jack's mouth was moving, but Cap couldn't make out his words.

He closed his eyes, counted to ten and opened them again.

"You okay, Cap?" Wade said, eyeing him with obvious concern.

"I'm fine," Cap said a little too sharply. *Get yourself together.* "Sorry. Eli is having some trouble with his schoolwork, and I guess I'm a bit distracted."

Way to go. Throw your kid under the bus to avoid admitting you have a problem. It was barely eight o'clock and this day was already getting off to a stressful start.

"You caught the part about the beauty pageant, right?" Jack said, scooping a perfectly formed omelet out of his skillet—a two-ton cast-iron monstrosity that no one else at the firehouse was allowed to touch, much less put in the dishwasher.

The back of Cap's neck went hot. "Beauty pageant?"

They had to be talking about Melanie. What had Cap missed?

"For kids." Wade poked at the omelet with a fork, claiming it as his own.

Jack sighed and went to work cracking more

eggs. A farmer on the outskirts of town dropped off a dozen or two at the firehouse every few days. The farmer's kindness was the saving grace that had allowed Cap to talk Jack out of building a chicken coop out back, behind the station.

"Felicity is all worked up about it. She wants to enter Nick." Wade's eyes went soft, the way they always did when he talked about his five-month-old son. "Although she insists it's not a beauty pageant, per se."

"What is it, then? A scholarship competition?" Jack snorted. "For infants and toddlers?"

Cap had no clue what they were talking about, but he had an irrational urge to defend Melanie... even though it sort of sounded like she wanted to throw a Miss Lovestruck pageant? For children?

That couldn't be right.

"What am I missing here?" Cap reached for the remains of his lemon-blueberry muffin, then thought better of it and crossed his arms.

He really needed to stop thinking about Melanie. And talking about her. And doing chores for her, like he was her boyfriend. Or her bae.

Did kids even say *bae* anymore? Cap felt ten million years old all of a sudden.

Jack and Wade exchanged an amused glance.

Cap frowned. "What?"

"We *know*, Cap," Jack said, tossing a pinch of salt onto the eggs on the stove.

Cap arched an eyebrow. Of course, they knew he'd been spending time at Melanie's house. There would probably be an article about it on the front page of the *Bee* this morning. "Whatever you think you know, you're quite mistaken."

"So you haven't been doing chores for the Miss America that just moved to town?" Wade asked, making zero attempt to hide the amusement in his eyes.

"Her name is Melanie Carlisle," Cap said, somehow refraining from mentioning that she wasn't just a former Miss America. She was a former *famous* Miss America. He was pretty sure her face had been on a lunch box at some point. It had come with a thermos that had a lid shaped like a lemon. "And it was just a one-time thing."

"But you were out there two days in a row," Jack countered.

"A one-time thing that just happened to be spread out over two days." A calculus formula probably existed that would have backed him up, but clearly no one in Cap's household knew what said formula might be. "We barely exchanged words. She definitely didn't mention anything about a children's beauty pageant."

"Well, it's happening. It's all anyone at The Bean can talk about." Wade picked up his paper coffee cup for apparent emphasis.

"Yep, I'm pretty sure Madison was teaching Emma and Ella how to wave like Queen Elizabeth yesterday," Jack said.

Wade shook his head. "Miss America's wave is nothing like Queen Elizabeth's."

"Yes, it is." Jack kept a firm grip on his spatula with one hand and moved the other back and forth in a stiff, closed-fingered wave.

"Nope. That's the queen wave. It's stiffer than a beauty-pageant wave." Wade set down his coffee cup. "Miss America waves like this."

Cap rolled his eyes as Wade mimed waving, dabbing away imaginary tears and straightening a tiara all at once.

"And you two are mocking the moms that hang out at The Bean?" Cap said. He needed coffee—bitter and black, none of the maple froufrou stuff everyone in town seemed to be drinking.

He headed toward the coffee maker, turned his back on the other two men and jammed a filter into place.

"Ask Miss Lovestruck about the pageant next

time you're over at her cottage 'doing chores,'" Wade said. Cap didn't need to turn around to know that he'd put annoying air quotes around the words *doing chores*. He could practically hear them, even above the dull roar in his head. "I'm sure she'll tell you all about it."

Cap gritted his teeth. He wasn't sure why their teasing about Melanie bothered him so much. The guys at the department always joked around like this, and Cap had always been as good-natured about it as anyone else.

But that had been before. Now...

Now he wasn't sure how much longer he'd be able to hang on to his position as fire captain and start his mornings with casual banter in the firehouse kitchen. He felt like everything he loved was slowly slipping through his fingers, and there wasn't anything he could do to stop it. And on top of it all, his kid was struggling at school.

Cap aggressively scooped coffee grounds into the filter from the enormous canister the firemen bought once a month at the discount store up in Burlington. "I won't be asking Melanie Carlisle anything because I won't be going over to her cottage anymore. Like I said, she's a complete stranger. If she weren't, I'd probably tell her that a pageant for children is probably the most absurd idea I'd ever heard. It's the last thing Lovestruck needs."

He flipped the coffee maker to the on position as Jack cleared his throat.

"What? Both of you know it's insane." Cap wiped his hands on a dish towel and turned around, fully expecting to find the other two men nodding in agreement.

But that's not what he found at all.

The first thing his gaze landed on was a pile of lemon squares, sprinkled with powdered sugar and neatly arranged on a ceramic platter decorated with—what else?—painted yellow lemons. Cap's gut churned. *Oh, no.* And then his gaze traveled from the platter of lemon squares, up the lovely, slender arms that were holding the tray, to the crestfallen face of Miss Lovestruck herself, Melanie Carlisle.

Melanie's smile froze in place. She didn't dare show Cap or the other two firemen how rattled she was.

Perhaps she should have. Maybe she should have taken one of the lemon squares and thrown it straight at Cap's stunned face. It probably would have felt amazing…

Not for long, though. Years onstage had taught Melanie to never, ever lose her composure. She'd survived all sorts of humiliating moments during her pageant career, from dropped batons to minor wardrobe malfunctions, and she'd never once let her smile waver. She wasn't about to start now.

"Good morning," she said, nodding at Cap before turning her attention to the other two men, who both looked like they were doing their best to blend in with the woodwork. "Sorry to interrupt. I just wanted to drop these by."

She moved to place the platter of lemon squares onto the counter, feeling completely and utterly ridiculous. She hoped Cap choked on a puff of powdered sugar when he tried to eat one.

"Just a thank-you for the work you did on my fence," she said by way of explanation. *Given that I'm a total stranger and all.*

Melanie felt her smile wobble ever so slightly. Ugh, stupid pregnancy hormones. There was no reason to feel so disappointed by Cap's brutal assessment of her. He was right. They didn't even know each other. The fact that she suddenly felt like crying had to be the baby's fault.

She was too old for this. When glowing young women with petite little baby bumps cried over silly things, they seemed sweet and vulnerable. When a woman in her forties did it, she seemed unhinged. At least that's how Melanie felt at the moment. Unhinged. And a little but furious, too.

The platter landed on the counter with a startling thud. The two firemen whose names Melanie still didn't know both gave a start. Cap just looked at her with a sadness in his eyes that scraped her insides.

Do not *feel sorry him. You're the wounded party here*, she told herself.

"Melanie, I'm so sorry." He frowned a frown so deep that she had to look away. "I didn't hear you come in."

She focused intently on the lemon squares. They were gooey and delicious. Melanie had consumed three of them as she'd been arranging them on the platter—again, the baby's fault. She couldn't seem to stop eating.

"No worries," she said brightly. "I probably should have knocked or something."

Instead, she'd sauntered right through the open garage door and into the firehouse as if she belonged there. Which she clearly didn't.

"Actually," one of the other firemen said, "a fire station is public property. It belongs to the taxpayers. You're welcome to stop by anytime. No lemon squares necessary."

He gave Melanie a kind smile, and she felt a little bit less like crying. She glanced at the name stitched on the pocket of his T-shirt and noticed that it said *Cole*—the same last name as Madison's.

He must be Madison's husband. She'd mentioned a family at home, but since Melanie's thoughts these days were so baby-centric, she'd been more interested in hearing about Madison's twin baby girls than whoever she might be married to.

Marvelous. Melanie felt tiny beads of sweat break out on her forehead. She had a grand total of two friends in Lovestruck, and by lunchtime today, they'd probably both know all about this mortifying lemon-square episode.

"Speak for yourself. I love lemon squares," the other fireman said. He winked at Melanie. "I also love brownies. Casseroles, too."

Melanie laughed, despite the warmth in her cheeks from the heat of Cap's quiet gaze.

"Ignore Wade here." Madison's husband removed a skillet from the stove top and slid the most exquisite omelet Melanie had ever seen onto a plate. "He just misses being showered with casseroles and baked goods now that he's a family man."

Wade grinned from ear to ear. "Worth it, my friend. I'd take Felicity and Nick any day over chicken and wild rice."

Felicity and Nick? Melanie wanted to crawl underneath the kitchen island and hide. *Both* of her new friends' husbands had a front-row seat to this embarrassment. Maybe she should just pack up and move back to Dallas.

Except the members of the Lovestruck Fire Department seemed awfully nice—not including Cap, obviously. Had she really been so misguided that she'd thought they'd had a connection? Yes, she had. She might have even thought there'd been a spark of attraction between them, fool that she was.

"Wade Ericson." The casserole-loving fireman offered Melanie his hand and tipped his head in the Madison's husband's direction. "This is Jack, and you already know Cap."

Melanie shook his hand and despite every effort not to, her gaze flitted in Cap's direction. Try as she might, she couldn't get his sharp voice out of her head.

I won't be asking Melanie Carlisle anything because I won't be going over to her cottage anymore...a pageant for children is probably the most absurd idea I'd ever heard. It's the last thing Lovestruck needs.

What could he possibly understand about pageants? He might know his way around a sledgehammer, but when it came to Melanie's world, Cap was clearly no different than the handful of other judgmental people she'd come across who thought everything she stood for was a frivolous waste of time.

Her heart thumped hard in her chest. She knew the best course of action would be to explain that the event she had in mind would be a charitable endeavor and a fun way to bring the families of Lovestruck together and give the children a chance to shine instead of whatever "absurd" spectacle he was imagining. Or maybe she should just forget about the pageant altogether.

But Melanie didn't want to forget about it. Felicity and Madison were excited about the event, and so was she. As Cap had so brutally put it, he was nobody to her. A total stranger, which meant she didn't owe him any sort of explanation. Proving him wrong might even be fun.

"Actually, Cap doesn't know me at all," she said.

Then she gave the men a flippy little wave before she spun on her heel and walked back across the street to her boutique.

Chapter Five

No one said a word after Melanie left the fire-house. Jack and Wade seemed to concentrate intently on their omelets while Cap just stood there letting his coffee get cold and feeling like the world's biggest jerk.

Was it crazy that he'd wanted to go after her and explain?

Probably—especially because there wasn't a thing he could say to make things better. He couldn't blame this particular faux pas on his tinnitus. Granted, he'd had his back turned and hadn't realized she'd walked into the building, but he suspected that Melanie wouldn't buy that as an explanation. Cap wouldn't have blamed her. He shouldn't have said anything behind her back that he wouldn't feel comfortable saying to her face.

Cap had always lived by that particular rule. It was simple, common kindness. His unchivalrous behavior this morning didn't actually have anything to do with Melanie at all. He'd seen her on the Miss America stage back in the day. He'd even read her book. Back then, Melanie had stood for optimism and positivity, and he had no reason to believe any of that had changed. Those were good lessons for kids—important lessons, especially in today's world. But, of course, he'd belittled her plans before he'd even heard what they were about.

Maybe it wasn't that bad.

Cap glanced up from his coffee. Neither of the other two firefighters would look him in the eye.

Definitely bad. Roger that.

He cleared his throat. "I have to drive to Burlington early in the morning, so can you head up the shift for the first part of the day tomorrow, Jack?"

Jack nodded. "Sure."

"Are you making a run up to the hospital?" Wade asked.

It was perfectly valid question. The general hospital in Burlington was the closest major medical center, and as such, when Engine Company 24 got pulled in on traffic accidents on the main highway or assisted the Burlington Fire Department with any large-scale calls, Cap had reports to prepare. Most of the time, he just completed the paperwork online, but occasionally, he needed to attend meetings and talk to other first responders, medical personnel or social workers face-to-face.

Not this time, though. This time, Cap's visit to Burlington tomorrow morning was personal.

"Something like that, yes," he said, shifting his gaze to the platter of lemon bars. They looked fantastic, and every time he breathed in, he inhaled the sweet, lemony scent that always seemed to cling to Melanie's hair.

Cap's stomach growled. He didn't dare indulge himself. Not even a bite.

"Anything we can help out with?" Jack said quietly.

Just tell them.

Cap took a deep breath. Jack and Wade were like his flesh and blood. He'd seen them through their own personal issues on multiple occasions. Cap had backed up Wade when he wanted to adopt the baby that had been left at the station last Christmas and he'd stood by Jack after his wife bolted, leaving the man to raise twin infant girls all on his own. He trusted these men with his life.

But this was different. If he couldn't learn to adapt to what was happening to him, his job would be at stake. Once he let the cat out of the bag, he wouldn't be able to reel the truth back in.

Still, keeping it bottled up inside clearly wasn't doing him any favors. And did he really want to keep something a secret when it was so fundamentally important to the station?

No. No, he didn't.

Cap lowered himself onto one of the kitchen bar stools and chose his next words with care. "Actually, there is some—"

An alarm sounded from the dispatch desk, situated just a few feet away.

"Got it." Wade tossed his fork onto his plate and went to check the monitor.

Jack tossed the dishes in the dishwasher, slinging water everywhere in case they had to head out in a hurry. The air in the firehouse was thick with adrenaline, and Cap's impending personal announcement was all but forgotten.

"It's Fancy," Wade said flatly. "Again."

Jack went pale. "You're kidding."

Cap stifled a grin. Fancy—a fluffy, cantankerous cat that belonged to longtime Lovestruck resident Ethel Monroe—had a habit of climbing to the tip-top of the sugar-maple tree in Ethel's front yard. Unfortunately, Fluffy hadn't quite mastered the art of climbing back down. The department had to rescue her at least once a month, and it was never a pleasant experience. Once, Jack had ended up hospitalized with a concussion. Hence his current state of visible panic.

"You swore to go out on every Fancy call for six months after everyone at the station signed up for Felicity's yoga classes," Jack said, narrowing his eyes at Wade. "Remember?"

"I certainly do. And that was six months, one week and three days ago. Your turn, my friend." Wade picked up his fork again.

"Both of you go. Brody will be here shortly. I can hold down the fort by myself until then," Cap said. Why not send the two men on the cat-rescue mission together? He was feeling nostalgic...and still a little out of sorts. Maybe if he had half a second of alone time, he could get his act together. "Perhaps there will be less blood-shed if it's two against one."

"Or perhaps that cat will kill us both," Jack muttered as he headed toward the apparatus bay.

Wade lingered for a moment, regarding Cap thoughtfully. "You never finished what you were about to say earlier."

Cap waved a hand. He was about to say "no big deal," but that would be a lie, wouldn't it? "It can wait."

A muscle in Wade's jaw ticked. They'd been through a lot together, particularly the last year or so. Cap wasn't fooling anyone around the fire station. "You sure you're okay, Cap?"

"I'm better off than you two are right now." Cap felt himself smile as he jerked his head toward the rig, where Jack was already suited up and ready to go. "Tell Fancy I said hi."

After Melanie closed up shop for the evening, she made the short walk from her boutique to Pages on Main, Lovestruck's independent book-store. She wasn't sure what to expect since she'd never set in foot in the place before, nor did she know exactly why she was there. Felicity and Madison had summoned her to the bookshop via group text, and as appealing as a hot bubble bath and a night in front of the Hallmark Channel sounded, Melanie just couldn't say no.

The two women were her only friends in town at the moment. She was beginning to wonder if they might end up being her only friends in Lovestruck. *Ever.* So Melanie didn't exactly have the luxury of turning down their invitation, even though for once in her life she didn't feel like shopping—not even for books, even though she'd always been an avid reader. What were the odds that Pages on Main had someplace where she could just put her feet up for a bit?

Listen to yourself, you sound, well...geriatric.

She'd let Cap McBride get under her skin. That was Melanie's real problem, and it made her furious...mainly with herself. Melanie had never been one to wallow. Lemons to lemonade, after all.

It was just that sometimes it seemed like she'd squeezed so many metaphorical lemons in her life that she just couldn't do it anymore. Lemonade was—dare she think it?—overrated. What she really wanted was a nice, big glass of wine.

But, oh, joy, that was also impossible. Not that Melanie would have traded her so-called delicate position for a sip or two of cabernet. Of course she wouldn't. Not in a million years.

"Melanie, hi! Over here!" Madison waved at Melanie as she pushed through the door of the bookstore.

But she lingered on the threshold for a second, getting her bearings. Pages on Main wasn't at all what Melanie expected. Sure, there were books pretty much everywhere. The walls consisted of whitewashed bookshelves with swirly crown moldings, and farm-style tables were clustered around the front of the shop, piled high with the latest hardback bestsellers. But a bar stood at the center of the space, propped up by dense stacks of repurposed antique books. Votive candles in Mason jars flickered from every nook and cranny, and the surface of the bar appeared to be covered in pages from old books. A sign wrapped in twinkle lights with the word *Uncorked* printed across it hung from ceiling, directly over the tall stools where Felicity and Madison sat waiting for her.

"Is this an actual wine bar? Right here in the middle of the bookstore?" Melanie said as she took a seat between them.

"It is," Felicity said. "Smoothie bar by day, wine bar by night."

"This is about the extent of the nightlife here

in Lovestruck." Madison waved a hand at their surroundings.

"I love it." Melanie grinned, feeling a bit better already. "But I might have a glass of milk, if that's okay?"

"Of course." Felicity lowered her voice to a whisper. "Is it terribly rude to ask when you're due?"

"Not at all. Five months." Melanie held up a single jazz hand. "And it's a girl."

Felicity's face lit up. "A future Miss America!"

Melanie laughed. "We'll see. I'm going to let her make that decision."

Pageants were definitely a family affair. Melanie's mom had been a pageant girl, as had her grandmother. Most girls who competed did so because their mothers had also participated in pageants and either had fond pageant memories, or wanted their daughters to be poised public speakers and learn community service and leadership skills—all very important things that the pageant system placed great emphasis on. But pageantry was also a big commitment and Melanie definitely didn't want her daughter to feel pressured to go as far as she had in the system.

The bartender slid a frosty serving of milk toward Melanie…in a martini glass.

"I repeat—I *love* this place," Melanie said and took a big, cold sip.

"Good." Felicity nodded.

"But this isn't just a social visit." Madison arched an eyebrow and exchanged a look with Felicity.

"It's a planning session," Felicity said.

"A planning session," Melanie echoed as she placed her glass back down on the bar.

Another wave of exhaustion washed over her. She knew where this discussion was going, and she wasn't sure it was someplace she wanted to revisit. Not anymore, anyway.

"For the pageant," Felicity said brightly.

Melanie took a deep breath. "I don't know. I've given it some thought, and I'm just not sure Lovestruck is ready for a children's pageant, even one focused on charity."

Felicity's face fell.

"But you were so excited about it yesterday." Madison frowned. "Don't tell me this is because of what happened earlier."

Felicity cleared her throat. "Um, Madison."

Melanie rolled her eyes. "It's okay. You two have already warned me that Lovestruck can be rather intimate." The world's biggest understatement, as far as Melanie was concerned. "I know that you both probably know all about the lemon-bar incident. Both of your husbands were there. If you hadn't heard, I'd be shocked."

"You're right. We heard," Madison said, wincing. "But you're not seriously considering abandoning the pageant idea just because of what Cap said, are you?"

Melanie sighed, ashamed to admit the truth. She'd been in the pageant world for practically her entire life. She was used to naysayers. Ordinarily, she'd never let one person's opinion get her down. Hearing Cap mock her behind her back had stung, though. She wasn't even sure she wanted to think about why it had upset her so much, but it definitely had.

"Possibly." She swallowed hard. "I've got kind of a lot going on right now—new house, new boutique, plus a new baby on the way. Maybe it's just too much."

Or maybe *she* was too much.

Greg's voice rang in the back of her head the way it did sometimes when she least expected it.

You're kidding, right? Sweetheart, you're not really cut out for a baby. Crowns and picket fences don't exactly mix.

He'd gestured to her closet when he'd said it, as if somehow her collection of evening gowns meant she wasn't mother material. Melanie had broken up with him on the spot. Eleven years of her dating life, right down the drain.

"If you've changed your mind because you have too much on your plate, that's one thing. But if you're having second thoughts about the pageant because of what Cap said, that's another matter entirely." Madison frowned into her glass of pinot grigio.

Felicity glanced at her and nodded. "It's weird, though, right? Cap usually isn't like that. He's one of the kindest people I know. He's the last person I'd expect to be so casually judgmental."

Madison nodded. "I was just thinking the same thing."

"Maybe he's right." Melanie swallowed. "Maybe a pageant really is the last thing that Lovestruck needs…or *wants*."

Maybe Greg was right, too, and crowns and picket fences truly didn't mix. Which meant she'd just uprooted her life for a hopeless cause.

Had she really thought she could just get rid of a fence and all of her insecurities would vanish right along with it?

Madison glanced at Felicity. "Show her."

Felicity grinned and fished around in her

giant Birkin bag, pulling out her phone. "Look at this."

She handed the phone to Melanie. It was open to Felicity's Instagram account, where she'd posted the photo of herself wearing Melanie's crown.

Melanie read the caption that Felicity had typed beneath it out loud. "'There's a new queen in town! Beauty queen Melanie Carlisle has taken over Blush Boutique on Main Street and her shop is as charming as can be. Who thinks she should put together a kid's pageant right here in Lovestruck?'"

Melanie set the phone on the bar and pushed it away as if it might burst into flames. If it did, the fire department would be the absolute *last* number she would dial.

"I'm afraid to read the comments," she said. Wasn't that the cardinal rule of the internet? Don't read the comments! People could be truly terrible from behind a computer screen.

Even more terrible than the things they say behind your back.

At least Greg had had the decency to insult her to her face, unlike a certain fire captain.

She reached for her milk while Felicity

cleared her throat and began reading the comments out loud.

"'What a fun idea!' 'Absolutely!'" Felicity beamed at Melanie. "This one is my favorite— 'The actual Melanie Carlisle?! She's always been such an inspiration. She could teach our kids so much about positivity and resiliency. This will be great for Lovestruck!'"

Melanie blinked. "Someone wrote that?"

"Not just someone," Felicity said, pausing for dramatic effect. "Diane Foster."

"She's basically the queen of the Lovestruck moms. She can be a bit of a gossip, but she runs the mommy circuit around here," Madison said by way of explanation. "Trust me. If she thinks the pageant is a good idea, everyone will."

Not everyone, Melanie told herself.

But she was finished letting Cap get inside her head. Standing inside the fire-station kitchen and hearing him dismiss the pageant idea as absurd and somehow denying that he even knew her had made her feel the same terrible way she'd felt when she'd had the baby conversation with Greg—as if she were a frivolous excuse for a person. Or, worse, a potentially bad mother.

Apparently, it was going to take a lot more

than just getting rid of a picket fence to help her move past her painful breakup.

"So what do you think?" Madison said.

Melanie felt herself smile. "I think the best lesson I can teach any child, especially my own, is to stay true to yourself. So, you're right. What difference does it make what a certain cranky firefighter thinks? Let's do this."

Get ready, Lovestruck. And get ready, Cap McBride.

Melanie was about to bring her particular brand of sparkle to this sweet little town.

Chapter Six

Cap's appointment the following morning was with an auditory therapist his doctor recommended.

Cap didn't have much downtime in his life—seriously, how did grown adults find the time to date? It was a mystery he couldn't begin to fathom. Not that he wanted to fathom it. Just the thought of it made him edgy, which begged the question: Why was he thinking about it at all when it hadn't crossed his mind for the better part of a decade? But the modest amount of spare time he did have lately had been occupied by Google searches. Along with his ill-fated attempts to teach himself calculus online, he'd done a very thorough internet investigation of his medical diagnosis.

Cap knew better. Everything sounded ten times worse online than it did in real life, but he couldn't help himself. Doom-scrolling NIHL for an hour had eventually led him to the conclusion that he needed to get himself enrolled in some sort of auditory therapy. So he'd emailed his general doctor in Lovestruck and requested a referral, after which he'd somehow landed on a grainy YouTube video of Melanie Carlisle's citrusy talent routine in the Miss America pageant.

He'd watched the video an embarrassing number of times by now, including while sitting in the parking lot outside the hospital as he waited for his appointment time with the therapist. There was just something really soothing about Melanie's bright voice and her reassurances that something wonderful could come out of even the saddest of life's moments. Lemons to lemonade. Cap was also oddly fascinated by the fact that she could squeeze the heck out a lemon while wearing a ball gown. At long last, he understood the appeal of the bizarre relaxation videos that Eli and his friends liked to watch. Maybe Cap wasn't as hopelessly out of touch as he thought he was.

"There are two different types of treatment I'd like to try in order to help you adapt to your condition," the therapist said, holding up two fingers and peering at him over the tops of her glasses. "Both are forms of sound therapy."

Cap nodded. "Sounds good. I am all for trying anything that might help."

The therapist, Dr. Ward, smiled at him. "The most common form of therapy for tinnitus sufferers is to create a quiet background noise that can be played on your nightstand while you're sleeping and, eventually, downloaded onto a portable device."

"I don't understand how adding more sound to the mix will help," Cap said, instantly deflating. The roar in his ears was constant. He needed less noise in his head, not more.

"This sort of sound therapy will provide a distraction to the ringing in your ears. It also helps desensitize you to internal noises and retrains your brain to pay more attention to external sound." The therapist smiled at him, as if retraining his brain seemed like the easiest thing in the world.

It sounded complicated and far more time-consuming than Cap had anticipated. He was forty. His brain was probably pretty set in its ways.

"What's the second type of treatment you thought I should try? You mentioned there were two, right?" With any luck, the second option wouldn't involve teaching one of his old-dog body parts completely new tricks.

"The other treatment involves focus exercises. I'll play a variety of sounds, one after another, and afterward you'll have to indicate which was the loudest, the longest, the highest or the lowest. We'll do this once a week. Again, the goal is to learn to focus on external sounds rather than internal sounds." Dr. Ward handed him a pair of headphones.

Cap took them. "So we're starting right now?"

"Right now." She nodded. "Just do your best. This isn't a pass-or-fail situation. It's practice. The more time you spend learning to focus on external sound, the easier it will become."

For the next twenty minutes, Cap made every attempt to ignore the dull roar in his head and instead listen to various sounds produced by string instruments, bells and keyboards. He was grateful it wasn't an actual test, because he was certain he would have failed. At first, it was impossible to tell which sounds were the loudest or the longest. Everything sounded the same, and just about all of it gave him a headache.

But by the end of the session, things started to click. He wouldn't have described his progress as a breakthrough by any stretch of the imagination. More like baby steps, but Cap would take what he could get. For the first time in months, he actually felt hopeful.

"Excellent work today. Does the same time next week work for you, Captain McBride?" Dr. Ward nodded as she tapped away on an iPad.

"Yes, it's fine. Is there anything I can do at home to help things along in between sessions?" Cap hoped so. Once a week didn't seem very often. Fancy got stuck in her tree with more frequency than that.

"Certainly. I'm going to prescribe the noise machine for you to situate beside your bed at night, and you can also repeat the focus exercises at home. You don't need to listen to the same types of noises we used today. Just pick a sound that you find pleasant and work on playing it for small stretches a time. Practice listening to it for five minutes, concentrating on it as hard as you can. And then increase the time by a minute or two every few days. Understood? I can recommend some recordings if you prefer."

Melanie's YouTube video sprang immediately to Cap's mind. Her comforting words. Her sweet voice, laced with just a hint of a Texas accent. All those lemons.

Cap cleared his throat. "I'm sure I can find something."

"Very well. See you next week." Dr. Ward scribbled something on the top page of a prescription pad, tore it off and handed it to him.

Cap took it and stood. "Thank you."

He left Dr. Ward's office with the closest thing to a spring in his step that he'd felt in a very long time. At long last, things were looking up. Cap waved at people he passed in the hospital corridors as he headed toward the elevator bank. He held a door open for a wheelchair-bound patient entering one of the many medical offices. He felt like his old self again instead of the irritable, distracted mess that he'd morphed into of late.

When the elevator doors swished open, Cap stepped inside and checked the time on his phone. The morning shift at the station had started a half hour ago. As long as traffic wasn't too bad, he should get to work by nine thirty or ten. Jack was a pro. He could handle things in the meantime.

And then, just because his phone was already in his hand and Cap knew that all he had to do was press the little red YouTube icon and Melanie's soothing voice would fill up the tiny space in the elevator, he started playing the lemonade video again. He tried to use the techniques he'd just learned in his therapy session to focus intently on her words, every musical lilt of her voice. He listened so hard that he never even heard the elevator doors slide open at one of the floors.

Cap wasn't sure why he looked up, exactly. All of a sudden, he felt swept up in a cloud of sugared lemon, like sunshine in a glass. He chalked it up to the power of suggestion, as onscreen, Melanie moved her wooden spoon in graceful circles, stirring her lemonade.

Still, he glanced up, anyway, and when he did, his heart nearly stopped.

"Hi, there," Melanie said, glancing down at his phone, still blaring her old Miss America video at full volume, and then back up at Cap.

She was standing right next to him, inside the elevator.

In the flesh.

And Cap had made an utter fool of himself, yet again.

When the elevators doors swished opened on the floor of Melanie's obstetrician's office and she saw Cap McBride standing inside, her first instinct was to flee.

His head was down, bent over his phone, so maybe if she moved fast enough, she could duck out of the way and wait for the next elevator. Maybe she'd even take the stairs. She might have decided to proceed with her pageant plans despite his unsolicited opinion on the matter, but Melanie still felt a sting of humiliation every time she set eyes on the man. And she most definitely didn't want to be trapped in a small, confined area with him. Not even for the short time it would take to travel from the fourth floor to the hospital lobby.

But then she'd heard a voice from the past— *her* past—and she'd frozen in place.

What on earth was Cap doing at the hospital in Burlington? And *why* was he watching a video of her twenty-year-old self making lemonade while journeying from floor to floor?

Curiosity got the best of her, so she'd lifted her chin and waltzed into the elevator as if she were wearing an invisible crown. The look on Cap's face when she said hello had been absolutely priceless—worth ever flutter of every tiny butterfly wing currently flitting around her belly.

Ugh, she couldn't possibly have butterflies. Maybe the baby was doing jumping jacks or something—tingly, romantic jumping jacks that made Melanie feel all swoony, like when she'd stood at her kitchen window and watched Cap tear down her idyllic white fence. Funny, she must have missed that chapter in *What to Expect When You're Expecting.*

"Melanie." Cap's eyes went comically huge.

Melanie would have laughed if she hadn't been so distracted by the conflicting emotions coursing through her like a roller coaster flying off its rails.

He jabbed at his phone. The volume grew louder, young Melanie's voice filling up the elevator car with the sort of unbridled optimism and naivete that Melanie had a much harder time mustering up after two decades of adulthood, before Cap successfully managed to pause the video and jam the device into one of the pockets of his firefighting cargo pants.

He closed his eyes for a beat and sweat broke out on his forehead. Melanie hadn't seen anyone look so uncomfortable since the time one of her students had dropped a flaming baton in the semifinals of the Miss Armadillo pageant. She almost felt sorry for him.

Emphasis on *almost*.

He opened his eyes, and Melanie had to give him credit for meeting her gaze full-on. Did his irises really have to be such a warm, welcoming shade of brown?

"Fancy meeting you here," he said, lips curving into a lopsided grin. "I was just studying up on how to make lemonade."

Sure he was. "So I noticed."

The elevator doors slid closed, and all at once, the small space felt far too intimate. Melanie turned to face front, but she could feel heat emanating from him. When she breathed in, she caught the scents of crisp mountain air and woodsmoke coming from his clothes. She had a sudden craving for s'mores.

She spun to face him again. "What are you doing here, anyway?"

He blinked. "I, um, had a doctor's appointment."

He offered up the slip of paper in his hands as evidence. It looked like a prescription.

"All the way in Burlington?" Melanie said. What was she *saying*? Why should she care why Cap McBride was seeing a doctor at a major medical center instead of the cozy little general practitioner's office in Lovestruck?

Except maybe there was something wrong with his health, like *bad* wrong. She was still mad at him, but she certainly didn't want anything bad to happen to him. In fact, just the thought of it made her heart beat hard in her chest.

"You're okay, aren't you?" she blurted.

"Yes," he said automatically and looked away. Then his brow furrowed, and he glanced back at her again. "I'm having some trouble with my hearing and it's causing me problems at work… and just in general. This morning I had my first appointment with an auditory therapist."

"Oh." Melanie went still. She had the ridiculous impulse to reach out and rest gentle fingertips on his forearm. She had to ball her hand into a fist to stop herself. Was this why he'd looked a bit lost when she'd found him in the hammer aisle, staring blankly at the neat rows of tools on the wall? "I'm sorry to hear that."

Her mind kept spinning back to the few moments they'd spent together. So much made sense now, especially the way he'd been so worried about coming too close to her with the sledgehammer when he hadn't heard her walking up behind him with the glass of lemonade. And his unanswered cell phone—clearly, he hadn't heard it ringing.

"I'm sorry, too," he said quietly. "Not about the hearing thing, but about what I said at the fire station."

Melanie blinked and resumed staring at the numbers on the elevator display as they moved from floor to floor. She'd kind of thought they were just going to ignore that embarrassing incident.

"Apology accepted," she finally said.

"Are you here about the baby?" he asked with a smile in his voice.

Her hand went automatically to her belly and she smiled back at him. She did *not* want to like this man, but with his honesty and unexpected sincerity, he was making it awfully hard at the moment.

"Yes. It's a girl. Weekly checkups are one of the joys of a high-risk pregnancy, apparently."

A muscle in Cap's jaw ticked. "High-risk?"

Melanie took a deep breath. *Nothing like near strangers sharing intimate medical details in a public elevator.* She didn't hesitate to elaborate, probably because he'd been so up-front about his own reasons for being there. "Because of my advanced age."

"Advanced age?" He arched an eyebrow. "Hardly."

And there went the butterflies again, swarming like crazy.

She arched an eyebrow right back at him. "Well, you're probably getting the actual me confused with that twenty-year-old version of me who you were watching on your phone just now."

The elevator dinged its arrival at the ground floor. *Finally.*

"Touché, Miss America." Cap laughed as he held the door open for her. "Touché."

Chapter Seven

Three days after Cap ran in to Melanie in the hospital elevator, the platter she'd hand-delivered to the firehouse sat on Lovestruck Engine Company 24's kitchen counter, mocking him.

The lemon bars were long gone, obviously. They'd lasted no longer than a single shift. For days afterward, the scent of lemons hung in the air, even though Jack, Wade or Brody had washed the pretty ceramic platter until it sparkled. Jack, probably. He was good at that sort of thing. Wade's sense of domesticity extended to Felicity, their five-month-old son and their ridiculously spoiled, senior-citizen Cavalier King Charles Spaniel, Duchess, and that was about it. He wasn't exactly the tidiest fireman in the department. Brody was great with a mop, a broom and a vacuum, but the kitchen was really Jack's domain.

He'd stopped short of walking across the street and returning the platter to Melanie, though. Cap couldn't fault him for it. She'd made the lemon bars for him, so he should be the one to return the dish. He just hadn't gotten around to it.

Right. Because walking across the street takes so much effort.

Okay, fine. Somewhere between running the fire department, doing his auditory exercises, searching for a math tutor and popping in on lacrosse practice to check on Eli, Cap could have found the time. But the more days that passed after their awkward elevator ride, the more daunting the prospect of seeing Melanie again became.

He certainly wanted to see her. Cap wanted to see Melanie again so bad that he'd begun daydreaming about her at the most inopportune moments. One minute, he'd been in the middle of a phone call with the fire chief for rural Vermont, and the next, he'd been remembering the way that sunlight brought out the golden highlights in Melanie's strawberry blond hair. His fingertips tingled just thinking about it. He wanted to bury his hands in those fiery curls so badly it hurt.

Never going to happen.

Of course it wouldn't. Things were complicated, to say the very least. Melanie was expecting a baby. He doubted that romance was anywhere on her list of priorities. It certainly wasn't on his, which was a good thing since he'd developed a really annoying habit of embarrassing himself every time he was in Melanie's presence.

She'd caught him watching her lemonade video. In a hospital, of all places. She probably thought he was some weird sort of stalker. If the same thing had happened to Eli, he would have begged Cap to transfer to a different school.

But Cap wasn't an insecure teenage boy. He was a grown man—some might even say a heroic grown man, given his chosen occupation. He could certainly muster up the courage to return an empty plate.

"I'll be right back," he said to Jack, Wade and Brody, who were all sitting around the kitchen table, poring over the latest edition of the *Lovestruck Bee*.

The three men exchanged amused glances as Cap snatched the platter off the counter.

"Don't say it," Cap grumbled. Whatever they were thinking, he didn't want to hear it.

As Cap looked both ways and strode across Main Street, he didn't dare look over his shoulder. Jack, Wade and Brody were probably sipping their cups of coffee and watching him from the station's big bay window. Sometimes the family-type atmosphere of a firehouse wasn't such a great thing. Privacy? What the heck was that?

In the short time since Melanie had taken up residence in Lovestruck, the children's shop had undergone a major transformation. The old, peeling sign out front had been replaced with candy-striped awning, dotted with little white bows. Swirling lettering on the front window spelled out *Blush Boutique*, with a lacy crown painted over each of the capital *B*'s. It was all very polished and feminine. Very *Melanie*, in a way that made Cap smile, despite the nerves coursing through him that made him feel like he was a boy about to ask a girl to prom instead of an adult male with a sudden craving for lemon bars.

A dainty bell tinkled when he pushed through

the door, announcing his arrival. Every head in the boutique swiveled in his direction.

Felicity, Madison and Madison's aunt Alice, along with several ladies from the knitting group that regularly attended classes at Alice's yarn shop, were all seated in a circle of white folding chairs near the cash-register area. He'd obviously interrupted a meeting of some sort.

"Good morning, ladies." He nodded, glancing from face to face until his gaze landed on Melanie, and all at once, something shifted inside of him. Like a long-forgotten memory rising to the surface.

Little Nick, Felicity and Wade's five-month-old son, was cradled in Melanie's embrace. The sight of her with a baby in her arms, coupled with her modest baby bump and the warm, peaches-and-cream glow of her exquisite face, took Cap straight back to a time when fatherhood was a new and wondrous thing. His throat grew thick. It had been so long since Cap had been in Melanie's place—awaiting the arrival of a tiny person that would change everything from that point forward. He'd forgotten what a beautiful and special time that had been.

"Hello, Cap," she said, smiling at him as the baby cooed.

Say something. He swallowed hard. *Or at least stop staring at her like she's a Madonna and Child painting.*

"I have your platter," he said stiffly, holding it up as if he were a salesman on the home shopping channel.

What was wrong with him? He administered CPR and saved people's lives with less difficulty than it took to have a simple conversation with this one woman.

"Thank you." She nodded at the counter, which was occupied primarily by an antique cash register painted white and decorated with intricately fashioned pink roses. Finally, a relic older than Cap himself. "You can just put it down over there."

"Sure thing." He walked over to the counter and set the plate beside a Lucite box like the ones his dad used to use to display his collection of signed baseballs. Except this box contained a crown, not a baseball. It glittered so much beneath the bright lights of the shop that Cap was afraid to look directly at it, lest it blind him.

He wondered if it was *the* crown. The one she'd eventually won by squeezing all those lemons. It had to be.

"Cap, since you're here, maybe you can help us with something," Madison said.

Doubtful, unless the smoke alarm needed new batteries. Cap felt distinctly out of his element at the moment, especially considering that half the female population of Lovestruck was observing every move he made.

Melanie shook her head. "I'm sure Cap is busy. I doubt he has the time—" she gave him a very pointed look "—or the inclination to volunteer for the children's pageant."

So he'd unwittingly crashed a meeting about the pageant, because, of course, he had.

Madison waved a hand. "I'm not asking him to volunteer."

Thank God and all that is holy, Cap thought.

"I just thought that since Cap is so involved with the community, he might have a suggestion for our charity project," Madison said.

Felicity sat up straighter in her chair. "Oh, what a great idea."

Even Alice angled her head toward him and nodded. "Indeed."

Cap itched to get out of there, but he couldn't turn down Alice Jules. No one in Lovestruck could. She could have asked him to knit a dog sweater right then for her Toby, her hairless canine, and Cap would have done it. It wouldn't have been pretty, but he'd have a made a solid effort.

"How can I be of assistance?" he asked.

Melanie lifted her chin. "Pageants always place a heavy emphasis on service, so we were just brainstorming different ways we could tie the children's pageant to a community charity project. But again, I'm certain you have more important things on your plate."

"More important than helping Lovestruck?" He crossed his arms.

He got it. He'd gone and stuck his foot in his mouth, and now Melanie had mentally cast him in the role of the big, bad pageant-hater. Never mind the fact that he was currently spending a laughable amount of time every day watching her Miss America talent routine. And never mind that he'd apologized. Good grief, he was never going to set eyes on another lemon bar, was he?

"Don't be silly," Felicity said.

"That's not at all what Melanie meant," Madison added.

Cap narrowed his gaze at the two women. Was there a chance at all that Wade and Jack hadn't been talking to their wives about their theory that Cap had a thing for Melanie?

Nope. Not a chance.

"We're trying to come up with a charity project that would fit perfectly with a children's event that's being hosting by an infant-and-toddler clothing boutique." Alice shot him a knowing smile. "You wouldn't possibly know about anything that fits that particular bill, would you?"

Cap sighed. How had he failed to see this coming? *Probably because you were too busy going all gaga over the sight of Melanie holding a baby.* He glanced her way again and an aching longing whispered through him.

Don't say it, he told himself. *None of this is your concern.*

He shrugged. "There's always the fire-department clothing drive."

Damn. He'd gone and said it.

Alice flashed him a wink.

"Perfect!" Madison gasped. "I totally forgot about that."

"What are you talking about?" Melanie glanced back and forth between Madison and Cap, wide-eyed. If her obvious state of alarm was any indication, she wasn't any more thrilled at the prospect of working on a charity project together than Cap was.

"The fire department has a children's clothing drive every spring. They get out in the community and try to get people to donate as many outgrown things as possible, especially winter coats," Madison said.

"Once it's over, we take everything down to the church. Come fall, the pastor distributes the items to families in need," Cap added.

"They try to make sure every child in Lovestruck has a warm winter coat before the cold weather sets in." Madison nodded. "Jack helped out with the project last year. He's been the chairman for several years running."

"It definitely sounds like the right fit for the pageant," one of the knitting ladies said.

"Absolutely. Mel, it's perfect!" Felicity clapped her hands. "You've got boxes of clothes you said you can't sell in the back storeroom. You can donate those to kick things off, and then every child who enters the pageant can bring at least one winter clothing item."

Madison flew out of her chair. "We could call it Crowns and Coats! I can do a write-up about it in my fashion column for the *Bee*. I'll bet we'll get donations from all over Vermont."

Melanie pressed her lips together. She looked as though she were trying her best not to smile. "It actually *does* sound like a good fit."

Cap met her gaze and his heart gave a zing. At long last, he'd done something right…even if it had taken a little nudge from Alice Jules.

"It's settled then." Alice nodded. "Melanie, your pageant can work together with the fire department on their annual children's clothing drive. Cap, you don't have any objections to calling the project Crowns and Coats this year, do you?"

As if he had any real choice in the matter. He could live with it, though. Especially if the added publicity increased the amount of cold-weather items they brought in. Winters in Vermont could be brutal.

He shook his head. "Nope."

"Wait." Melanie held up a hand. Nick reached tiny baby fingertips toward a pretty gold charm bracelet that dangled from her wrist. "Shouldn't we be running this past Jack? Since he's the project chairman on the fire department's end?"

"No need." Cap shook his head.

Melanie narrowed her gaze at him. "Why not?"

Madison shrugged. "He's not the chairman this year."

Melanie's cheeks went as pink as her pretty striped awning out front. She was beginning to catch on, apparently. "Then who is?"

Again, all heads swiveled in Cap's direction.

He raised his hand. "You're looking at him."

Why did Melanie get the feeling that she'd been set up?

No, that wasn't possible. She was just being paranoid. A partnership with the fire department's children's clothing drive was truly a perfect idea. But why, oh, why, did Cap McBride have to be the chairperson?

She tried to forget about that most inconvenient detail as the meeting continued, with Madison volunteering to use her resources at the *Bee* to design posters and fliers to display around town, and Felicity promising to tell her Mommy and Me yoga class all about the pageant. Alice's knitting ladies couldn't wait to enter their grandkids. They would hold the pageant a month from now, which gave them just enough time to get ready. Then Melanie could take things easy as she entered the third trimester of her pregnancy. Everything was falling perfectly into place.

Well, almost everything. Melanie bounced Nick in her lap as she watched Cap walk back across the street, toward the firehouse. Was she imagining things, or did there seem to be an extra spring in his step all of a sudden?

She knew he couldn't be happy about being roped into working with her on the clothing drive. Melanie was fairly certain he'd been pressured into it. If there hadn't been an unmistakable twinkle in his eye when he'd announced that he was the new chairperson for the clothing-drive committee, she would have thought she needed to go back to the drawing board and come up with another idea.

Apparently, though, he intended to see things through. Melanie didn't know what to think or how to feel about it…the annoying butterflies fluttering around in her tummy notwithstanding.

"I think we're finished for today, unless anyone has questions?" Melanie said.

The shop had already been open for a couple hours and foot traffic was beginning to pick up, so she needed to get back to actual work, even though Melanie could have talked about pageant stuff all day long. Her mom hadn't known what she started with she'd given Melanie that Miss America lunch box back in first grade.

"I think we're good. The mayor has agreed to let us hold the pageant in the town square. We can use the gazebo as a stage, which should make the kids feel comfortable since they've pretty much all grown up here," Alice said.

Madison's aunt was a miracle worker—sort of like a town mom. She had a lot of pull in Lovestruck.

"I'm creating an online entry form. It should be up and running by the end of the day," Felicity said as she glanced at the time on her phone. "Oops. Nick and I have to run. I've got a yoga class starting in fifteen minutes."

Melanie gave the baby a kiss on his soft little head and passed him over to Felicity. "Thanks for letting me hold him awhile."

"Anytime. We're all family around here."

Melanie's heart gave a little squeeze. *Family.* That's precisely the type of life she wanted to build here in Lovestruck. Her mom and dad had both passed away years ago, and being an only child, Melanie didn't have much family left— just some distant cousins who lived halfway across the country. In recent years, the pageant girls she coached had been the closest thing to an actual family that she'd had in a long while. And Greg, of course. Or so she'd thought.

"See you ladies next week for another meeting," Alice said, and when she headed off to her yarn store, her knitting group followed en masse.

Maybe Melanie should learn how to knit. Craft projects had never been her strong suit. She was more comfortable twirling a baton than holding knitting needles, but things could change, right?

Madison helped Melanie put away the white folding chairs they'd set out for the meeting, and then a hush fell over the quaint shop after everyone had left. Melanie dragged one of the boxes of outdated inventory from the storeroom to the cash-register area so she could go through it and set aside coats for the clothing drive. She'd accumulated a nice pile of puffer coats and baby flannel when a red-haired woman pushing an ergonomic stroller walked into the boutique.

"Good morning," Melanie said. "Welcome to Blush."

"Aren't you the sweetest? Good morning," the woman said and then pressed her hand to her heart as she spotted the dinosaur display. "Everything here is just precious. You've really done a wonderful job reinventing this old place."

"Thanks so much. It's a work in progress, but I'm trying to get things all settled in the next few months." Melanie patted her baby bump. She was, after all, on a deadline of sorts. And she still needed to find someone who could hold down the fort at Blush in the weeks after she gave birth.

The woman plucked a stegosaurus onesie off the rack and carried to the register. "Of course you are. When are you due, exactly?"

Melanie had never felt quite comfortable talking about her pregnancy back in Dallas. Trying to sidestep questions and correct assumptions that the baby was Greg's had *not* been fun. Both of those things had definitely contributed to her decision to move. She'd wanted a fresh start, and she had zero intention of telling anyone about the sperm bank. The last thing Melanie wanted was for her child to hear about his or her conception from a total stranger. She wanted to have that conversation when the time was right, and if the news was common knowledge, such a plan just wouldn't be possible.

In Texas, keeping the details of her pregnancy under wraps would have been next to impossible. Here in Lovestruck, things were different. Not a single person had pressed her for information about her past. Other than the infamous lemon-bar incident at the fire station, the town had pretty much welcomed her with open arms.

"I'm due in five months," she said as she rang up the onesie on the antique cash register and folded it gingerly in a layer of pale pink tissue paper.

"Oh, lovely. Just in time for the Lovestruck pumpkin festival."

Lovestruck had a pumpkin festival? Of course it did.

Melanie felt herself smile as she took the woman's credit card. When she glanced down, she noticed the name on the Mastercard seemed familiar.

Diane Foster.

Oh, right! How had Madison described her, again? Queen of the Lovestruck moms.

Melanie did her best not to glance at the crown sparkling away in its Lucite box.

"So where's the father?" Diane said in a tone so saccharine-sweet that Melanie's teeth practically hurt. Even a maple latte from The Bean would have seemed bitter by comparison.

"I'm sorry, what?" Melanie said, stalling for time.

"The baby's father." Diane tilted her head and flashed a bright grin. A casual bystander would probably have described it as a beauty-queen smile, but Melanie knew better. There was nothing authentic or wholesome about it. "From what everyone's saying, you're here on your own. How terribly sad for you and your baby. It's such a shame."

"It's fine, actually," Melanie said. "*We're* fine. Wonderful, even."

She shoved the bag containing the dinosaur onesie toward Diane, hating the way her hands had started to tremble.

"Of course you are. And we're all so happy to have you here in our quiet little town." Diane took the bag.

Melanie shoved her hands behind the counter, out of view. *Breathe, just breathe. Pretend you're onstage waiting for the top finalists to be announced in a national pageant. Don't let her see you sweat.*

"But where did you say the father was, again?" Diane's eyelashes fluttered. The toddler in her stroller started to squirm.

"I didn't," Melanie said. "He's not in the picture. It's just us."

Please leave. Just take your Jurassic fashion and go.

"I hope you don't my asking about him. It's

just that everyone in town is wondering about it, and no one wants to come out and mention it out loud." Diane took hold of the stroller and aimed it toward the door. "See you soon. We're all so excited for the pageant."

Melanie tried to come up with a polite response, but for once, words failed her. And then Diane trilled the most dreaded words of all as she exited the boutique.

"Bless your heart."

Maybe things in Lovestruck weren't falling so perfectly into place, after all.

Chapter Eight

"I really don't understand why we have to do this door-to-door." Melanie peered up at Cap as they walked down one of the streets in Lovestruck's historic district. Her eyes were huge pools of bottomless emerald green.

If Cap didn't know better, he'd have thought she was terrified.

"We don't *have* to," he said, glancing down the neat row of cottages.

A stack of fliers for the Crowns and Coats clothing drive was in his hand. It featured a logo of a fire engine, topped with a gigantic tiara. The plan was to go door-to-door, chat with the residents and let them know about the clothing drive and that the Lovestruck children's pageant was working in coordination with the Engine Company 24 to collect winter coats for kids in need. A week before the pageant, a child and his or her family from the event would be coming by to collect donations.

Melanie had been quite adamant about the kids being the ones to collect the coats and bring them to the fire station. She wanted the pageant to instill a spirit of volunteerism in the children, even the young ones. Cap had zero arguments. In fact, he thought it was a fantastic idea.

On the other hand, Melanie definitely seemed less than thrilled about his plan to kick things off by knocking on doors.

"It's just that every year the firefighters go door-to-door and ask the residents to consider donating to the drive." He shrugged. "It's kind of a tradition around here."

"Then I guess we have to." Melanie squared her shoulders. "I definitely don't want to be the newcomer who rolls into town and turns all the local traditions upside down."

Cap figured it wasn't a good time to mention that Melanie had sort of already done that very thing by starting a pageant in the first place. Anyway, it was too late to put a pin in things now. In the twenty-four hours since the pageant had been announced, the entire town had gone tiara crazy. Cap couldn't set foot outside the firehouse without hearing about talent routines or "fancy dress."

Actually, scratch that. The same conversations were taking place right inside the fire station. Jack's toddler twins and even Wade's five-month-old baby, Nick, had been among the first kids to "sign up" for the pageant. Cap had no clue what a baby was supposed to do for a talent routine. According to Jack, a parent was supposed to "help" the tinier kids with their performances, which explained why he'd seen Diane Foster tap-dancing in her driveway yesterday afternoon.

Cap still didn't get it. Again, Wade and Jack had tried to fill him in. In addition to helping a child feel more poised and comfortable in social settings by appearing onstage—or in the case of Lovestruck, on gazebo—for a minute and half in front of a supportive audience, the pageant was also supposed to be a bonding experience between parent and child. A family event. In any case, he had a feeling he hadn't seen the last of Diane Foster's tap shoes.

Cap planted his hand on the small of Melanie's back as they approached the first house. It was a gesture born of habit—Cap's attempt at gentlemanly behavior. But the instant his fingertips came into contact with the softness of her polka-dot dress, an electric spark passed through him. Casual contact with Melanie felt anything but casual, and when he heard Melanie's sharp intake of breath, he could only assume that she felt it, too.

Melanie rang the doorbell and they both faced forward. Cap concentrated as hard as he could on the home's brass door knocker and the wreath hanging just above it, decorated with sunny yellow flowers and sugar-maple leaves. But all he could think about was Melanie's worried expression.

Something was wrong. He wasn't sure what could have happened in the day and a half since he'd last seen her, but if Cap could have seen inside Melanie's lovely head, he had a feeling it would be spinning with ripe, uncut yellow lemons. Not lemonade.

"Hello?" The door swung open, revealing

Cap's high-school math teacher, Evelyn Hughes. "Oh, hi there, Jason. It's so nice to see you."

Her gaze swiveled toward Melanie, flitted briefly to her baby bump and then back to Melanie's face. "Isn't this a surprise? Please introduce me to your special friend."

Melanie shook her head so hard that Cap thought it might snap right off her neck. "Oh, no. He's not—"

"We're not—" Cap said at the same time.

Evelyn's eyebrows crept closer to her hairline.

Cap sighed and shoved a flyer into her hands. "We're here about the children's clothing drive. The fire department is working with the Lovestruck children's pageant to find coats for kids in need."

He somehow stumbled through an explanation of Crowns and Coats while Melanie stood silently beside him, beaming like a Miss America contestant. Anyone looking at her probably wouldn't have noticed that the smile didn't quite reach her eyes.

Cap did, though. Maybe it was his repetitive viewing of her lemonade video, or maybe, little by little, he was actually getting to know her, despite the fact that their limited interactions had all been contenders for the awkward hall of fame. In either case, he could tell she was uncomfortable. Beneath all of that beauty-queen polish, there was a vulnerability that Melanie kept to herself. There wasn't a doubt in Cap's mind that she could do anything on her own that she set her mind to. She'd taken the world by storm at the tender age of twenty. The woman was a sunshiny, lemon-bright force to be reckoned with.

But Cap didn't want her to have to take everything on all by herself. She was going to have a baby. He knew firsthand how hard being a single parent could be. Melanie deserved to have someone by her side, especially now. That probably made Cap old-fashioned, but so be it. He was beginning to realize that he was developing good old-fashioned feelings for the beauty queen across the street.

Friendly feelings, he told himself. *Nothing more.*

Sure, because he always listened to recordings of his friends' voices for therapeutic reasons.

"Do you think you might have access to some children's winter clothing to donate to the Crowns and Coats drive?" he asked, even though he'd begun to lose track of what he'd been talking about. Yet another problem that didn't seem altogether platonic.

"Of course. I keep coats around the house for my grandchildren. They outgrow them every year and I get them new ones. I'll bundle the old ones together and have them ready when the children come by to pick them up," Evelyn said.

"Thank you so much." Melanie gave her a regal nod. "We really appreciate it."

They bid Evelyn goodbye and the moment the door shut, Melanie's smile crumbled.

She turned toward Cap. "This is just what I was afraid of. It's true, isn't it?"

Cap's gut churned. He didn't want Melanie to be afraid of anything, least of all his old math teacher. "I'm not following."

Melanie grabbed him by the hand and dragged him off the porch and down the sidewalk, until they were positioned beneath the cool shade of a magnolia tree. Pillowy white flowers bloomed overhead, enveloping them in sweet floral perfume.

Melanie leaned toward him and whispered in his ear, "Is it true that everyone in town is speculating about the father of my baby?"

"No," Cap said. Granted, he'd wondered about it, just a little bit. Mainly because he didn't want to think that she'd been running away from an abusive relationship or anything. New job, new town, new life.

Just the thought made him sick to his stomach, but he didn't dare ask. Clearly the topic wasn't up for discussion, and Melanie was safe here in Lovestruck. If necessary, Cap would make certain of it.

"Not one person has asked me who the father of your baby might be," Cap said.

"Well, of course they haven't." She rolled her eyes. "They think it's you."

Cap felt himself frown. "Not possible."

"Obviously." Melanie laughed…a little too loud. "We don't even know each other. Not really."

Don't we, though?

Cap's jaw clenched. He'd told her his deepest darkest secret. The truth had come tumbling out of him in the elevator at the hospital. She knew things about him that no one else did—not his friends and coworkers, not even Eli.

But how could Melanie possibly know that? Cap hadn't even told her that his hearing problems weren't public knowledge. He hadn't had to, apparently. She hadn't breathed a word about it to anyone. If she had, Cap would have heard all about it by now.

"Maybe it's time to change that," he said quietly.

Her eyes grew wide again, like he was about to ask her to keep knocking on doors. Or, worse, stick a white picket fence in her front yard.

"Come on." He strode down the sidewalk, back in the direction they'd come. The clothing drive could wait. Or maybe they'd buck tradition and announce it in the *Bee* instead of canvassing the town. Sometimes change could be a good thing.

"Where are we going?" Melanie said, falling in step beside him.

Someplace where they were sure to be invisible. At least, in Cap's experience.

"Trust me, Miss America."

"Lacrosse." Melanie's gaze slid toward Cap, who was sitting beside her on a checkered picnic blanket. "I have to admit that I know nothing at all about this game. Texas is tailgate parties and Friday night football."

She was sure that people played lacrosse in Texas. They must have. She'd just never witnessed it with her own eyes.

"It's Lovestruck High's most popular sport. Eli lives for it. That's him at the far end of the field." Cap pointed to a lanky boy with the number twenty-three stitched onto his practice jersey. He was doing what looked like a running-and-catching drill with one of his teammates, as they tossed a ball back and forth with their sticks. So far, lacrosse reminded Melanie a lot of hockey.

Only instead of sitting in a cold, icy arena, she was currently nestled beside Cap on a blanket he'd spread beneath the shade of a covered red bridge.

Melanie had gasped out loud when he'd pulled his truck alongside the meandering creek behind Lovestruck High School. She'd yet to see one of Vermont's famous covered bridges, and she'd had no idea that there was one tucked away right here in Lovestruck. Best of all, the bridge was no longer in use, so it was the perfect picnic spot.

Melanie squinted at Eli, but he was too far away for her to see if he had his father's perfectly chiseled jaw or warm brown eyes. She could tell he was Cap's son, though, just by the way he carried himself. They had the same broad shoulders and the same slight swagger in their step. Like father, like son.

"He looks just like you," Melanie said.

Cap shot her a lopsided grin. "You can't possibly discern that from this distance. We're not anywhere near the field."

He was right. From where they sat, hidden in a shady corner of the weathered bridge, they could just make out the numbers on the players' shirts. It was just an after-school practice, not a real game. If it was, she had a feeling Cap would be situated in the front row of the bleachers that ran the length of the massive lacrosse field.

"Still, I can tell. You two move the same way." Melanie should know. She'd snuck enough glances at Cap from across the street as he moved about the apparatus bay. She could tell him apart from Jack, Wade and Brody just by the way he rolled up his shirtsleeves.

Which probably wasn't a normal thing to have noticed about a man she wasn't going to date. Ever.

She was finished with dating. If she hadn't gotten married and settled down by now, why on earth would she think things would change? *Crowns and picket fences don't exactly mix.*

She swallowed. Hard. "I think it's sweet that you come here and watch him practice in the afternoons."

"Not every afternoon, just on my days off

from the station." Cap opened the lid of the wicker picnic basket he'd produced from the back of his truck once they'd parked beneath a cluster of sugar-maple trees close to the bridge. "There's not much in here. Sorry, spying on my kid's lacrosse practice is usually a solo activity."

He offered Melanie a shiny red apple, and she took it. "Wait. Spying? Are you telling me that Eli doesn't know you do this?"

Cap shrugged. "I'm pretty sure he's spotted me over here on occasion, but we don't talk about it."

Melanie rolled her eyes. "I will never understand men. Why on earth would you think this needed to be an open secret?"

"Because I remember what it's like to be that age—lingering in that space between childhood and adulthood. I wanted to be independent and have my own life." He sighed. "But at the same time…"

"You wanted to know there was someone there who would catch you when you fell." Melanie nodded.

She knew all about the push and pull he was describing. She'd lived it with the teenage girls she'd coached. One minute, they'd nail the personal interview portion of a pageant, speaking eloquently about everything from gun control legislation to—yes—world peace. Then seconds later, tears would be streaming down their faces because a friend hadn't texted them back or because they'd lost some little trinket they'd carried to the pageant for good luck. Melanie had wiped away teenage tears every bit as often as she'd bobby-pinned tiaras in place. It came with the territory.

"In Eli's case, it's not so much falling as failing. He's having some trouble with academics, but we're working on it." Cap reached into the picnic basket and retrieved a bottle of water.

Melanie bit into her apple as she watched the muscles in his forearm flex when he twisted the cap. Since when did she get all swoony over a man's forearm?

"Enjoy the time you have with your little one when she arrives. It all goes by in the blink of an eye," Cap said, and suddenly there was a sadness in his expression that made Melanie's heart twist.

She nodded. "I will."

Their eyes met, and Melanie had the sudden urge to lean forward and press her lips to his. As if he could read her mind, Cap's gaze drifted slowly to her mouth.

Her heart pounded so loudly that it roared in her ears. She felt her lips part ever so gently... and then the apple in her hand tumbled out of her grasp and landed on the picnic blanket with a thud.

"Oops." She scrambled to pick it up.

What were they *doing*? This was supposed to be an innocent little break from volunteer work, not a romantic interlude.

Melanie's face went hot. It was the bridge's fault. Honestly, did it really need to be so charming and picturesque? She felt like Meryl Streep in *The Bridges of Madison County*, the movie that had been all the rage when Melanie was fifteen and competing in the Texas Junior Miss pageant. That summer, no less than eight girls performed monologues from the film during the talent competition. Meryl they were not.

Melanie clutched the apple to her chest as if it were a life preserver. "Thank you for bringing me here. It's really lovely, and you were right. There's no one around. The high-school kids are in their own world. It really is like we're invisible."

The corner of his mouth tugged into a half grin, and Melanie considered that maybe the covered bridge wasn't entirely responsible for the quiet intimacy that had formed between them. Maybe it had more to do with Cap than she wanted to admit.

He let out a low laugh. "Darlin', you couldn't be invisible if you tried."

Chapter Nine

The following day, Melanie got up bright and early for her weekly checkup with her obstetrician in Burlington. Although, did it really count as getting up early when she'd barely slept a wink?

She'd tried everything—all the usual tricks that typically helped quiet her mind and lull her pregnancy hormones to sleep. Chamomile tea, lavender-scented sleep spray, soothing lullaby music. She'd even tried counting sheep, but the longer she lay there with her eyes squeezed closed, the more those fluffy white lambs seemed to look like little balls bouncing back and forth between lacrosse sticks.

The picnic with Cap had been so unexpected, so *fun*. Melanie couldn't remember the last time she'd done something purely for fun's sake. Like most pageant girls, she was very goal-oriented. Sure, she usually had a great time along the way, but she was always striving toward something. Always anxious to take the next step. For the first time in her life, she was taking things slow and learning to live in the moment.

At least that had been the plan when she moved to Lovestruck. But the boutique needed so much work and then she'd decided to throw a pageant. She still hadn't hired anyone to take over at Blush when she went on maternity leave. Sometimes Melanie felt like she'd gotten off one hamster wheel and jumped straight onto another, albeit a hamster wheel with the added benefits of maple lattes, covered bridges and outrageously hunky firemen.

Somehow, though, when she'd been with Cap under the bridge, time seemed to move at a much slower pace. Like a wooden spoon moving lazily through a pitcher of chilled lemonade. At times, she'd wanted to rest her head in his lap and go to sleep.

This was bad. Very, very bad. Melanie should not be having these sort of feelings about a man right now. Particularly not about Cap. Granted, he'd apologized for the things he'd said about the pageant, but Melanie still wasn't sure where he stood on all of that.

Also, she was pregnant, just getting over a major breakup and had recently learned she was geriatric. Now was not the time to develop a crush on the local fire captain.

So she'd given up on sleep and headed to her moonlit backyard, where she'd plucked an armful of lemons from her tree. An hour and a half later, two dozen lemon melt-away cookies were packed into a Tupperware container for the staff at her doctor's office. Lemons to lemonade…or in this case, lemons to lemon cookies.

She felt better already, more in control of herself and her wonky emotions. She was *not* going to be one of those pregnant women who cried over every tiny thing or accidentally fell in love with a near stranger. Just because she was going to have a baby didn't mean she was going get "baby brain."

And then Melanie walked outside to head to her car and found Cap's truck parked at the curb. He waved at her through the unrolled window. One glimpse at that manly forearm and she melted on the spot, just like the cookies stacked inside the Tupperware container that she nearly let slip from her hands.

Cap hopped out of the truck and met her on the sidewalk—right in the spot where the swing gate to her picket fence once stood.

"Morning," he said, as if showing up at her cottage at 7:00 a.m. was the most normal thing in the world.

"Good morning." Melanie's heart thump-thump-thumped in her chest. "What are you doing here?"

"I figured since we both have weekly appointments at the exact same time in a city sixty miles away, we should probably carpool." He shrugged one shoulder. "It's the responsible thing to do."

Melanie nodded. "Good for the environment."

"Exactly. Less pollution," he said.

"Less carbon emissions," she added.

He tilted his head. "Less greenhouse gasses."

"I'm convinced." How could she refuse? Melanie did love the planet, after all.

Oh, please. Planet earth is the absolute last thing on your mind right now.

Cap held the door open for her as she climbed onto the passenger seat of his truck. It was just common courtesy—not date behavior in any way, because geriatric or not, Melanie had not gotten to the stage in her life where traveling to his-and-her doctor appointments qualified as romance. Still, another one of those inappropriate flutters coursed through her as he winked at her and shut the door.

She could do this. It was a car-pool invitation, not a marriage proposal. Melanie stole a cookie from the Tupperware and shoved it in her mouth as Cap jogged toward the driver's side of the truck.

He started fastening his seat belt and froze. "Do I smell lemon bars?"

Melanie wiped a crumb from her lips. "Lemon melt-away cookies. I couldn't sleep last night. Want one?"

He nodded. "Absolutely."

They sat in companionable silence as Cap maneuvered the truck past rows and rows of white picket fences until they merged onto the highway. The horizon before them was like a watercolor painting, all mist-covered mountains and shimmering green grass.

"This was a good idea," Melanie finally said. "It feels more like a road trip than a visit to the doctor. I'm less nervous than I was last week."

Cap glanced at her and then directed his attention back to the road. "Everything is okay with the baby, though, right?"

"Yes, thank goodness. Everything is fine, so far." Other than her age, which she wasn't going to mention again. Enough of that nonsense. At the moment, she was feeling anything but old.

"I'm glad." Cap nodded.

"Speaking of the baby, were you being serious yesterday when you said that not one person had asked you about the father?" She slid her gaze toward him, determined to figure out if he was simply trying to reassure her or if he was really being honest.

"I solemnly swear that no one has asked me that question." Cap's lips twitched into a grin. "They have, however, asked what you have against white picket fences."

Melanie laughed. Out here beneath the sweeping Vermont sky, her pile of whitewashed firewood and Greg's hurtful comments felt very far away. "I can see why that might be a topic of conversation."

She waited for Cap to ask her why tearing down the fence had been such an urgent matter, but he didn't. He seemed perfectly content to let her keep her secrets, which should have been a relief. Strangely enough, his patience had the opposite effect.

Melanie felt herself opening like a book. Cap had told her about his medical struggles, and she was almost positive that he hadn't shared that information with anyone else. He hadn't said it was a secret, but he hadn't needed to. She'd sensed it.

He'd also taken her to his secret picnic spot, and she hadn't shared a single real thing about herself with him in return. Just lemon bars and cookies.

Melanie cleared her throat and kept her gaze fixed on the horizon. She was so tired of looking backward. She didn't want to do it anymore. "It was because of something my ex-boyfriend said."

Beside her, Cap grew quiet. He didn't ask her to elaborate or to continue—he just gave her the time and space she needed to find the right words.

"We were together for a really long time. Years. And six months ago, when I told him I wanted to start a family, he laughed." Melanie's voice hitched, and Cap reached for her hand and squeezed it tight. "He said I wasn't cut out to be a mom and that crowns and picket fences don't mix."

The moment the words left her mouth, she felt like weight had been lifted off her. Why had she been keeping the awful truth inside for so many months? Saying it out loud took some of the sting out of Greg's words.

But maybe it was more than that. Maybe she'd needed to wait for the right time to say them—the right *person* to hear them.

"That definitely explains why I spent two days demolishing Lovestruck's newest picket fence," Cap said. "Mystery solved."

"I hope it wasn't too much trouble," Melanie said, grinning. She felt as light as air. And the memory of Cap tearing the fence apart, board by board, made her feel like laughing hysterically all of a sudden.

"Anytime, darlin'." Cap glanced at her, his eyes dancing.

Then her gaze met his, and his grin faded. The look on his face turned so sincere that all of her breath bottled up in her chest.

"Your ex couldn't have been more wrong. You'll be a wonderful mother, Melanie. I hope you know that."

The way he said it, with such calm conviction, stirred something inside her. She felt more like herself than she had in a very long time—not perfect and not without fault, but whole. Whole…and happy. As happy as a newly crowned beauty queen.

"I do," she said quietly.

And then her heart seemed to hold its breath.

I do…

Wedding words.

"Captain McBride?" Dr. Ward glanced down at the chart on her desk. "Tell me how the past week has gone. Have you set up the noise machine? And were you able to get some practice in on the focusing exercises?"

Cap nodded. "Yes and yes."

He was willing to do anything to adapt to his condition. Anything. So, of course, he'd followed all of Dr. Ward's instructions to a T.

Cap had been leery about how to explain the noise machine on his nightstand to Eli. He didn't want to worry his son, but he also didn't want to outright lie to Eli, either. Doing so would go against everything Cap believed in as a parent. Cap hadn't been a perfect father, but he'd always been honest. Even in the dark days after

Eli's mom died, Cap had always told five-year-old Eli the truth.

Daddy, I miss Mommy. When is she coming back?

She's not, son. I'm sorry.

Luckily, Eli was a teenager, which meant the last place he wanted to set foot was his dad's bedroom. The noise machine had taken up residence in the McBride household, completely unnoticed by the younger McBride.

"And have you noticed a difference in how your tinnitus has impacted your day-to-day life?" Dr. Ward offered him a kind smile. "Relative to the last time you were here, I mean."

"Not yet," Cap said. Again, honest to a fault. "But I'm feeling a bit more hopeful than I was the last time I was here."

"Good." Dr. Ward jotted down something on the chart.

Of course, Cap wasn't convinced that his auditory therapy had much, if anything, to do with his recent uptick in optimism. Probably it was a by-product of his chosen material for his focusing exercises. The heart of the lemonade video wasn't about lemonade at all. Multiple times a day, he'd listened to Melanie's sweetly Southern voice tell him that he might not be able to control the world around him, but he could control his reaction to it. Even in the midst of darkness, he could turn his face toward the light. He could believe in it—chase it, even—and create a life filled with hope and wonder. He could take his lemons and turn them into the sweetest, most delicious lemonade imaginable. Unexpected, unplanned, but everything he wanted—just not quite the way he'd always pictured it.

Or maybe Cap's rekindled hope had more to do with the messenger than the message itself.

Cap had watched the lemonade video so many times that he could recite Melanie's speech by heart. Sometimes he forgot he was supposed to be viewing it for therapeutic purposes, and instead, he just watched the way the stage lighting made the sequins on her evening gown sparkle every time she moved. Once, he'd become mesmerized by the graceful turn of her wrist as she stirred her wooden spoon.

Still, he hadn't entirely realized that he'd been developing feelings for Melanie until she'd looked at him yesterday like she wanted him to kiss her. Cap hadn't seen that particular look on woman's face in years—maybe even a decade— but he knew it when it saw it.

What he hadn't remembered was how alive it made him feel…

He'd thought he had things figured out. Days ago, Cap had decided that he and Melanie were like opposite sides of the same coin. They were around the same age and they lived in the same town, but they were moving in completely different directions. In so many ways, Melanie was just getting started. She had a new career, a new home and, in just a few months, she'd have a new family. A whole new life.

Cap, on the other hand, was winding down. For months, he'd had the strangest feeling that his life was slipping through his fingers. He didn't know what his NIHL diagnosis meant for his career. In just a couple years, Eli would be off to college. He wasn't sure how it had happened, but all of a sudden, his life seemed to be getting smaller and smaller. While Melanie was blossoming, Cap was doing the exact opposite.

But when her emerald eyes had gone dark and liquid, and her gaze had lingered Cap's mouth, it felt like the hands on all the clocks in Lovestruck had started spinning backward. Cap had been electrified. Full of life…and light, just like her old talent routine for Miss America.

Why shouldn't he bury his hands in Melanie's fiery hair and kiss her silly? It wasn't the craziest idea in the world. Sitting beneath the shade of the covered bridge while yellow daffodils swayed in the spring breeze, it had felt right. He wanted Melanie. He *needed* her.

When the apple had gone tumbling from her hands, the moment had passed, but they could get it back. Cap knew they could.

"Are you listening, Captain McBride?" Dr. Ward's clipped, professional tone broke through his thoughts, dragging him away from yesterday's picnic and back to the present.

"Sorry," he said. "What were you saying?"

She studied him through narrowed eyes. "Is your tinnitus bothering you right now? Is that why you didn't hear my most recent treatment recommendation?"

He considered her question. There was indeed a dull roar in his head at the moment, but his mind had been wandering. That's all. "It's not bothering me any more than usual. Again, I apologize. I was just thinking about something else."

Some*one* else—a strong, beautiful someone who would make a fantastic mom, regardless of what her idiot ex had told her.

"I understand." Dr. Ward nodded. "I'm glad.

For a minute there, I thought perhaps the mention of hearing aids had rattled you."

Wait.

What?

Cap went still—so still he thought his heart might have even stopped beating. *Hearing aids?*

He shook his head. "No."

"I realize you might not be ready right now, but it's something you should consider. An auditory device would amplify external sound and make it easier for you to discern external stimuli from internal stimuli."

"I thought that's what the focus exercises were all about." He tried to swallow but his throat had gone bone-dry. "And the noise machine."

"Correct, and we will definitely still put those therapies to use." Dr. Ward opened her top desk drawer, removed a brochure and slid it across her desk, toward Cap. "But nothing is going to work as well as a hearing aid can. I just wanted to bring it up so you can think about it."

Cap didn't need to think about it. It wasn't going to happen, plain and simple. He was only forty, for crying out loud.

But Dr. Ward didn't budge. She just sat there, waiting for him to do something with the brochure. So he took it, folded it in half and tucked into one of the pockets of his cargo pants.

"Captain McBride, the reason you're experiencing hearing loss is because you've been a firefighter for over two decades. It has nothing whatsoever to do with age." Dr. Ward's expression turned sympathetic, which only made Cap feel worse.

Intellectually, he knew she was right. He just wasn't ready to admit that his situation was that dire. In all his years of firefighting, Cap had never met an actively employed firefighter who wore hearing aids. Was that even acceptable protocol?

Cap truly didn't know, but one fact was already beginning to crystallize in his mind with frightening clarity: he couldn't hide a hearing aid. If he wore one, his worst insecurities would be on display for all the world to see.

Cap wasn't used to needing help of any kind. He'd always been the strong, stoic one—the backbone of his family, his fire station, his community. If Cap no longer looked like that person on the outside, he wasn't sure who he would be on the inside.

He balled his hands into fists as he went through the motions of the rest of his therapy session. He wore the headphones, did his best to tune out all the excess noise so he could focus on the sounds he was supposed to focus on. But somewhere in the background, he could have sworn he heard all the clocks in Lovestruck again—much like he had the day before.

Except the clocks weren't spinning backward anymore. They were keeping proper time, hands moving relentlessly around and around and around.

Tick.

Tock.

Tick.

Chapter Ten

"How are things going with Crowns and Coats?" Felicity peered at Melanie over the rim of her oversize coffee cup.

After nearly a month as an official resident of Lovestruck, Melanie was at long last experiencing the maple-scented joy of her first visit to The Bean. The town's favorite, albeit only, coffee shop sat proudly at the corner of the busiest intersection on Main Street. From her front display window at Blush, Melanie had seen the crowd of moms in matching athleisure wear that descended on The Bean every morning. After meeting Diane Foster in the flesh, she hadn't been in a hurry to join them. Or go anywhere near them, frankly.

But Felicity and Madison had gasped in horror when they'd heard that Melanie still hadn't experienced Lovestruck's finest gourmet coffee in anything but a "sad paper take-out cup," as Felicity had called it. So their next scheduled committee meeting for the children's pageant had been moved up an hour, before Blush opened for business. Now here they were, nestled into one of The Bean's plush booths while the rest of the Lovestruck moms gathered on the sidewalk out front to push their strollers on a power walk through the historic district.

Melanie looked up from the perfectly shaped maple leaf that the barista had artistically drawn into the foam of her decaf latte. "Crowns and Coats? Oh, fine. Everything is totally under control."

Spoiler alert: things were not fine. Neither were they under control in any way, shape or form.

Melanie wasn't sure how it had happened or why, but things with Cap had grown tense lately. He'd stopped calling her "darlin'" or "Miss America." In fact, he'd stopped flirting with her altogether, which should have been a relief since Melanie wasn't interested in a relationship.

Except she sort of was, so long as that relationship was with Cap.

"You and Cap finished going door-to-door?" Madison asked.

"Yes." Melanie sipped her latte. "I mean, no."

Felicity and Madison exchanged a glance.

Felicity tilted her head. Nick, sitting in his bouncy seat beside her, babbled and played with his feet. "Which one is it? Yes or no?"

"We decided to do things a little differently this year. Instead of going to door-to-door, we did a mailer. And remember, Madison, you did that story in your column for the *Bee*?"

Madison nodded. "Sure, and honestly, that will probably result in just as many donations as knocking on doors would have. Possibly more. I just didn't realize you'd switched gears. Cap is pretty big on tradition. I'm surprised he wanted to change things up."

Melanie nodded. "I was, too, actually." She frowned into her latte. "Anyway, we've got twenty children signed up for the pageant and they have a week to round up donations and drop them off at the firehouse. The station has probably already collected a good amount of coats."

"Perfect." Madison closed her planner, where she'd been jotting down notes from their meeting.

"I'm sure you and Cap plan to get together and do an inventory of the items coming in," Felicity said, smiling down at Nick and giving one of his feet a gentle squeeze.

Melanie loved watching Felicity and her son together. She took him nearly everywhere she went. Melanie had only met Madison and Jack's twin girls, Emma and Ella, a couple of times. They were adorable, and Madison dressed them in the cutest matching outfits, but twin toddlers weren't quite as portable as a tiny five-month-old. On the days that both Jack and Madison had to work, Jack's mom took care of the girls at home.

Hearing about how much energy and sheer manpower it took to manage a household with twins had alarmed Melanie to no small extent. What if her early ultrasound had been wrong and there wasn't just one baby growing inside her, but two? Or possibly even three?

But her doctor in Burlington had assured her that there wasn't a spare baby hiding in her womb. The galloping of her baby's heartbeat was the most wonderful sound that Melanie had ever heard, and it was also very much singular in nature. Thank goodness.

Melanie glanced out the window and down the block, where the shiny red ladder truck sat parked outside the firehouse. She and Cap did *not* have plans to go over the donations together. When she'd tried to set a time for them to sift through the items, Cap had said he didn't mind doing it himself. And then he'd said little else during their entire ride back to Lovestruck from the hospital in Burlington.

The only time Melanie had seen him in the flesh was the following Tuesday, when he'd shown up, as promised, to take her to the hospital for her weekly appointment. She'd made a lemon loaf topped with royal icing and sliced into neat rectangles. Cap hadn't eaten a single bite.

"You know what?" Melanie gulped down the remaining few sips of her latte and set down the mug with a clunk. "Yes, Cap and I are indeed going to go over the donated items together."

"Okay," Madison said, arching an eyebrow.

Felicity nodded. "Good."

"Right now, actually." Melanie slid out of the booth and stood before she could lose her nerve.

Was Cap *ghosting* her? That's what her students back in Texas used to call it when a boy they liked suddenly stopped communicating.

Technically, she supposed he wasn't, since he was still working on the committee and giving her rides into Burlington. But something had changed about the way he interacted with her. And the change had a definite Casper-like quality to it.

Madison and Felicity exchanged a look. They seemed confused, and Melanie couldn't blame them. As usual, though, they were supportive.

"Go, girl," Madison said.

"I am." Melanie nodded. "Going, that is."

Why weren't her feet moving?

Oh, right. Because she was about to go storming inside the firehouse, unannounced. The last time she'd done such a thing, it hadn't gone over too well.

Too bad. She missed the old Cap. Not the one who'd embarrassed her over a platter of lemon bars, but the other one—the one who reminded her of covered bridges and awkward elevator encounters. The one who'd told her she would be a good mother. The one who she still wanted to kiss, despite all her doubt and hesitation.

The Cap that had worked his way into her

heart was the sort of man who might even make her reevaluate her stance on picket fences.

But where had that man gone?

Cap sat at the farm table in the firehouse kitchen and stared down at the notepad in front of him. The pages were covered with numbers, x's, y's, t's and myriad symbols whose meanings remained a mystery.

Calculus was *not* an easy subject to master, no matter how many times a person read *Differential Equations for Dummies*. The only thing that was proving more difficult was locating a reliable tutor for Eli.

The first person Cap hired had been a college student from nearby Middlebury College. He'd been almost an hour late for his first session with Eli, and the second time, he hadn't bothered to show up at all. Apparently, there'd been a party at the tutor's fraternity house the night before. The tutor wondered if they could reschedule for an ambiguous time in the future after his hangover had worn off, and Cap had opted to decline.

His luck with online tutors hadn't been any better. There was only so much a person could explain over Zoom. Eli's homework grade had raised from a D to a C, but he'd still failed his most recent quiz. Cap needed to do something. Quick.

"You forgot to rewrite the terms so that each of the t's are in the numerator with negative exponents before taking the derivative," someone said in a familiar Texas drawl as a beauty-queen-shaped shadow fell across Cap's notebook.

Surely he hadn't heard that correctly. Cap's tinnitus was clearly playing tricks on him. Weird, math-related tricks.

He looked up, and found Melanie standing in front of him, furiously beautiful.

"Melanie." Was this real? Cap hadn't been sleeping much lately. But if this was a hallucination brought on by exhaustion, why did she sound like a math professor all of a sudden? "What are you doing here?"

"Hello to you, too," she huffed and then snatched his pencil from his hand.

She leaned over and began scribbling some indecipherable combination of letters, numbers and squiggles on the paper in front of him. Cap tried to follow the quick movements of her hands, but he got momentarily distracted by the gold highlights in her hair as waves of strawberry blondness spilled over her shoulders.

He took a sharp inhale to get his bearings. It didn't help in the slightest.

"See." She tapped the complicated string of numbers she'd just written on the notepad with the tip of the pencil's eraser. "*This* is your derivative."

It was like she was speaking a completely foreign language. Math had never sounded so appealing.

Cap gaped at her. "You know how to do calculus?"

"Of course." She crossed her arms. A charm bracelet with baby-themed charms dangled from one of her wrists. "Why wouldn't I? Do you think that pageant girls are somehow inherently bad at math?"

"Of course not," Cap countered. He thought *he* was bad at math. Far worse than Eli, even.

He flipped his *Differential Equations for Dummies* book closed so she could see the title. "The dummy in this scenario is me."

"Clearly." Her lips twitched into a reluctant smile before she resumed glaring at him.

Jack, Wade and Brody strode into the room, took one look at the two of them and promptly turned around and walked back out.

Super. Cap would definitely be hearing about

this later—and just when he'd finally put enough distance between himself and Melanie to quash his coworkers' questions about their relationship.

Not that they had a relationship. Cap had come to his senses in that regard. He and Melanie just weren't meant for each other. Period. The optics of him rocking a newborn infant in his arms while at the same time wearing hearing aids was just too much for him to contemplate.

Cap knew he was being prideful. Worse yet, he was being presumptive. But a man didn't spend countless hours thinking about kissing a pregnant woman without also thinking about taking care of her and her baby. Maybe even building a life with them. Not a man like Cap, anyway.

"Would you like to sit down?" he said.

"That depends." Melanie squared her slender shoulders. "Are you ghosting me?"

His answer was automatic. "No, of course not."

That's not what he'd been doing, was it? Because if so, wow. It went against everything he'd tried to teach Eli about respect and character.

The relief that splashed across Melanie's face made his chest ache. "Promise?"

"I promise." He stood and pulled out a chair for her. "Sit down. Please?"

"Okay, but only if you stop acting so strange." She lowered herself into the chair and rested a hand on her growing baby bump. Cap's throat grew thick. "I thought we were friends."

Friends.

The ache in Cap's chest grew deeper. He didn't want to be Melanie's friend. He wanted more. So much more. The realization hadn't fully dawned on him until this precise moment.

"We are," he said, voice going gruff with all the things he was trying his best not to say. "Of course, we're friends."

"I'm glad. I don't have a whole lot of friends around here, you know."

Cap felt like the biggest jerk in the world.

"But you will," he said. The whole town would be in love with her, sooner or later.

"Thanks for saying that." She smiled and the indignation in her glittering green eyes cooled into something resembling affection.

"It's true." He felt himself smile. "Now please tell me how you know so much about calculus— not because you're a 'pageant girl,' but because this stuff is impossible to understand."

He shoved the *Dummies* book toward her with a poke of his finger, and she laughed.

"It's really not that complicated, and I suppose I just have a head for it." She shrugged one elegant shoulder. "The girls I taught in my pageant coaching business were all required to maintain at least a B average in all their classes at school. Otherwise, I wouldn't let them compete. While we traveled to and from small provisional pageants, the girls did their homework and studied on the bus. I sort of ended up being a part-time tutor in addition to their pageant coach."

"That's amazing," Cap said. *She* was amazing.

She studied him for a beat. "Are you doing this for Eli?"

"Yes." He arched an eyebrow at the woefully incorrect calculations he'd written on the notepad and grinned. "Do you think it will help?"

"Not even close." She laughed, and then searched his gaze. Her words from a few minutes ago burrowed beneath Cap's skin. *I thought we were friends.* He wanted to kiss her right then and there to show her just how friendly he could be. "I could help Eli if you like."

"I would love that," Cap said. "I mean *we* would love that. Eli and me."

Melanie grinned. "How does tonight sound?"

* * *

Lucky for Eli, he turned out to be better at calculus than his father.

Once Melanie watched him attempt the first few problems on his homework assignment, she was able to identify the areas that were giving Eli the most trouble.

"See this?" She pointed to five equations he'd gotten wrong. "When you see radicals, you should always convert the radical to a fractional exponent first. And then simplify the exponent as much as possible."

The boy nodded, and his hair flopped over one of his eyes. Eli had eyes like his father—warm and friendly. Velvety brown.

"Oh." His face lit up as he tried one of the equations again. "I think I get it now."

"Good. I think if you remember that one rule, it will make a big difference going forward," Melanie said.

Happiness coursed through her as he went through the problems again, one by one. Other than a minor multiplication error in one of his proofs, he got every single one of them right.

"Dad, look. I'm doing it." Eli shot his father a goofy grin as Cap walked into the room.

Melanie and Eli had been sitting at the kitchen

table in Cap's cottage in the historic district for about an hour. Soon after they'd started working, Cap had made himself scarce, insisting that he didn't want to be a distraction.

She'd still been able to see him in the periphery, sorting the through the boxes of donated items for the clothing drive that he'd brought home from the firehouse. That had been their deal—he would work on the charity project, while Melanie helped Eli with his homework. Cap insisted he wasn't trying to "Casper her out of the clothing drive," but was just trying to distribute the work as evenly as possible since she was helping Eli purely out of the goodness of her heart.

Melanie was worried he was going to offer to pay her, which would have made her feel like an employee instead of a friend. After everything she'd said to him at the fire station, that was the last thing she wanted. Cap had apparently picked up on it, because he hadn't breathed a word about money. Instead, he'd offered her pizza and salad when she'd arrived at his house. She, Cap and Eli had sat around like a family, eating dinner and chatting about their respective days. A rebellious lump had formed in Melanie's throat. She still couldn't seem to make it go away.

"You're a miracle worker, you know that?" Cap said to her as Eli gathered his books and headed toward his bedroom.

"Thank you, Miss Carlisle," the boy said, grabbing a slice of cold pizza on the way.

"Anytime, Eli," she called after him. "And I'm Melanie, not Miss Carlisle."

"Seriously, you might have just saved his high-school lacrosse career," Cap said quietly.

Melanie had to stop herself from wrapping her arms around his neck and resting her head on his shoulder. Cap was back again. *Her* Cap, not the wooden man who'd taken his place lately.

He's not yours, she reminded herself. *And you don't want him to be.*

Why did that little nugget of truth keep slipping her mind?

"That's what friends are for," she said.

"Friends," Cap echoed, and the corners of his lovely mouth tipped into a frown.

He took a deep breath and seemed to weigh his next words carefully. "Do you have time to sit down and talk for a minute before you go?"

Melanie nodded. She didn't have a son waiting for her at home. Nor did she have an activities calendar like the one attached to Cap's refrigerator with a Lovestruck Lacrosse magnet. Or piles of schoolbooks and pizza boxes. Or shoes that had been kicked off by the front door and framed family photographs sitting on every available surface—all the things that made a house a home.

Cap raked a hand through his hair, then gestured toward the living room, where they sat down beside each other on his caramel-colored leather sectional.

He took a deep breath. "I wanted to explain why I've been distant lately."

Melanie held up a hand. "You don't owe me an explanation, Cap. It's okay. We're—"

"Friends," he said. "I know."

Why did the word *friends* seem unbearably sad all of a sudden? And why couldn't she seem to stop saying it?

Except she hadn't been the one to say it this time. He had.

"I was going to say we're fine." Melanie grinned at him, but her smile wobbled.

She wasn't sure she wanted to have this conversation, after all. She had a feeling where it might be going, and it definitely didn't seem pleasant.

He'd stopped flirting with her because she was pregnant, hadn't he? Her baby bump felt like it was leaving *cute* territory and heading straight for "oh, wow there's a baby in there." Pregnant women weren't supposed to date. Even Rachel on *Friends* had gone on a dating hiatus when she'd been expecting. Granted, that had been Ross's idea—*ugh*—but still.

"I'm glad we're fine." Cap nodded. "I guess I'm just going to come out and say it…"

Melanie braced herself.

Cap's voice went low. Serious. "My auditory therapist wants me to try hearing aids."

Melanie blinked. *Hearing aids?* That's why he'd gone all Casper on her? "Does she think they'll help?"

He nodded.

"Then I guess I don't understand the problem. Why wouldn't you want to give them a try?"

"I'm having a hard time wrapping my head around it, I guess. The suggestion took me by surprise, and I supposed I've been feeling a little…"

His voice drifted off, but he really didn't need to go on. All of a sudden, Melanie knew the exact word he couldn't seem to articulate.

Geriatric.

Welcome to the club. If anyone could relate, it was Melanie.

"Cap, it's not a sign of weakness. Or age. The problems you're having just mean that you've spent years helping people. It's an occupational hazard, nothing more." She reached for his hand and wound her fingers through his.

Friends did that sort of thing, right? Especially when one of them was hurting.

He squeezed her hand tight, then ran the pad of his thumb over knuckles until a shiver coursed through her in a most *non*friendly manner.

"I know you're right. I just need to set my pride aside, get used to the idea and talk to the other members of my department about it. And I will." He blew out a breath. "But not yet. I *know* I shouldn't feel embarrassed, but I guess on some completely asinine level, I do."

"Trust me, I'm familiar with that particular blend of contradictory emotions." Melanie cleared her throat and met his gaze. And then she said the words that she never in a million years would have said to Diane Foster. But this was different—this was Cap. There was no doubt in Melanie's mind she could trust him. "I went to a sperm bank. That's why I don't like it when people ask about the baby's father. It's personal, between my baby and me. Someday I'll tell my child all about it. The last thing I'd want is for her to hear it from someone else. Not that I'm not ashamed… I'm definitely *not*."

Cap's expression went tender—so tender that Melanie's throat grew thick and she realized she was looking at him through a veil of tears. "Of course, you're not ashamed, darlin'. There's no reason to be at all."

And then he cupped her face in his heroic hands. A tear slipped down her cheek, and he wiped it away with a gentle brush of his thumb. Melanie hadn't expected to share so much of herself with Cap, and while a part of her felt like she'd just taken her first real exhale since she'd moved to Lovestruck, another part of her—the part she thought she'd abandoned for good—seemed to be waking up, like a flower slowly unfolding and leaning toward the light. She'd never wanted to be kissed so badly in her life.

Cap's gaze swept her face, and his eyes bore into hers as if he were asking her an unspoken question.

Yes. Melanie nodded ever so slightly. *Oh, yes, please.*

And then just as her eyes drifted closed and Cap's mouth came down on hers, Eli called out from the kitchen.

"Dad? Where's the rest of the pizza?"

Chapter Eleven

The following day, Eli made a rare appearance at the fire station after school. Cap was in his office, filling out paperwork for the chief who oversaw the rural Vermont stations, when his son slapped a paper covered in pencil squiggles on his desk.

"Hello to you, too." Cap leaned back in his chair and grinned at Eli. He was starting to look so grown-up. Even the framed picture on the corner of Cap's desk that he'd taken during one of Eli's freshman lacrosse games last year looked woefully outdated.

"Hi." Eli gave him a lopsided smile and then pointed at the paper. "But seriously, Dad. Look."

Cap's gaze swept over the page. It was filled with equations that gave him a major flashback to his *Differential Equations for Dummies* book, which was buried at the bottom of one of his desk drawers, hopefully never to be seen again. But in the paper's top margin, a big A with a circle around it had been written in fat red Sharpie ink.

Cap looked at Eli. "No way."

"We had a pop quiz today, and I aced it. Can you believe it?" Eli flopped down in the spare office chair on the opposite side of Cap's desk. "Miss Carlisle—I mean, Melanie—really helped."

Cap nodded. "I'm sure she'd love to hear about this A. Her shop is right across the street. Maybe you should stop by and let her know before you walk home."

"I will." Eli grinned.

It had been a while since Cap had seen such unabashed joy on his son's face. It made him feel strangely wistful for something he couldn't quite identify—either the past, or maybe a future he was only beginning to think might be an actual possibility.

Eli leaned forward in his chair, forehead scrunching. "What's the deal with the two of you, anyway?"

"Um…" Cap redirected his gaze back down to the paper. He had no idea how to answer that question.

On the one hand, Eli had nearly walked in on Cap and Melanie almost kissing last night. But they'd sprung apart the second they'd heard Eli in the kitchen. Cap wasn't even sure why. It had just been an automatic reaction.

Maybe it had something to do with the number of years it had been since he'd kissed anyone. Cap definitely remembered how, but he wasn't sure he was ready for an audience, particularly if that audience was his fourteen-year-old son.

Plus, Melanie had pretty much fled immediately afterward. Cap hadn't even been able to get her to stay long enough to join him and Eli for reheated pizza. Weren't pregnant women supposed to be hungry all the time?

"Nothing is going on," Cap said, which was—sadly—all too accurate.

Eli's gaze narrowed. "So you're not dating or anything?"

"No." Cap refused to believe he was already

at the age where going to doctor's appointments together counted as dating. "We're friends."

That's what Melanie had kept saying over and over again. *Friends.* Cap had been wrong to nearly kiss her. The timing hadn't been right at all. She'd been vulnerable—crying, for goodness' sake. What had he been thinking?

He hadn't. For once in his life, Cap had gotten out of his head and let himself *feel* something. And what he felt for Melanie nearly knocked him off his feet.

"Friends," he repeated.

Although he wasn't sure the emphasis was for Eli's benefit or for his own.

Melanie kept herself as busy as she possibly could for the next couple of days. She worked on the final arrangements for the pageant and dealt with the huge influx of new customers who'd been eager to pay a visit to Blush and check out the new beauty queen in town. But more than anything else, Melanie worked at forgetting that Cap had almost kissed her.

It had been an achingly honest, vulnerable moment for both of them. The kiss had nearly been a mistake. Neither one of them had been thinking clearly. Eli's interruption had been a blessing in disguise.

That's what Melanie told herself, anyway. Because any other version of that strange, intimate conversation was just too much for her contemplate. She and Cap were both dealing with some major life changes. Could the feelings that either one of them were experiencing be trusted? Just a few days ago, he'd been avoiding her like the plague.

Melanie was on the rebound from a decade-long relationship. Her heart was still tender. She wouldn't—*couldn't*—let herself be hurt like that again. Not ever…and especially not now. Her baby came first. Every decision she'd made since she'd found out she was pregnant had been for the baby. She'd only just wrapped her mind around how to be a mother. Melanie had no idea how to be a mom and fall in love at the same time. It just didn't seem possible.

Who said anything about love?

No one had, and that was exactly the point.

After Cap arrived, Melanie sat beside him and chatted happily all the way to Burlington. She'd made lemon poppy-seed muffins, which were all but gone by the time they pulled into the hospital parking lot. Things between them had returned to normal. Melanie just wasn't sure what normal was anymore, or why it no longer seemed like enough.

"Good luck at your therapy session today," she said as they stepped into the elevator together.

"Thanks. I hope all goes well at your appointment." Cap held the door open for her when they reached her obstetrician's floor.

"It's just another routine checkup," Melanie said. "I'll see you afterward in the lobby. Right outside the coffee shop, as usual?"

She swallowed hard. Leaving him felt weird all of a sudden. Everything did.

"I'll be there." Cap flashed her a grin as the elevator doors slid shut.

Melanie took a deep breath. She was overthinking things, as usual. She'd assured Cap that they were fine, and they were.

Everything was fine.

Until it wasn't.

Cap arrived at the coffee shop first, which wasn't unusual. His therapy sessions always started and ended precisely on time. Melanie's appointments weren't always as predictable, since her doctor was an obstetrician and sometimes got called away to deliver babies.

He scrolled through his phone, checking for any texts and emails at the fire department. Everything at work seemed fine, so he read a few articles from the online edition of the *Bee*. Madison had mentioned the upcoming pageant again in her fashion column, so Cap copied the link and texted it to Melanie, along with a quick message.

You're going to like Madison's column today. I'm ready and waiting in the lobby whenever you're finished. Grabbing you a mineral water. Lemon-flavored, obviously.

He stood in line, bought Melanie's water and a black coffee for himself and then checked his phone to see if she'd texted him back. Nothing. Not even any of those flashing dots that meant someone was typing a message.

Cap frowned down at the small screen. He glanced at the time in the upper left-hand corner. He'd been waiting for twenty minutes. A ribbon of unease wound its way through his consciousness.

Twenty minutes isn't really that long in the scheme of things. She'll either text back or walk off the elevator any second.

But then twenty minutes turned into thirty, and thirty turned into forty. Cap had begun to pace back and forth in front of the coffee shop, eyes glued to the elevator bank. By the time the forty-five-minute mark rolled around, his sense of unease had crystallized into cold, hard panic.

Something was wrong. If she were just running late, Melanie would have sent him a message. Intellectually, he knew that there were other potential explanations for the radio silence—a dead phone battery, for instance—but deep in his gut, something just didn't feel right.

Cap couldn't just keep standing there, waiting. He was going to give himself a coronary. Even though the hospital would have been the most convenient place possible to have a heart attack, that just didn't seem like an advisable course of action. Cap really had no choice.

He was going to have go and find Melanie.

Cap jogged to the elevator and pressed the button for the floor where she always bade him goodbye. The short ride seemed to last an eternity, but it wasn't until the doors slid open and Cap burst out of the elevator that he realized he didn't know her doctor's name.

This wasn't good. Not at all. Why had he never thought to ask her for this information?

She was a single mom-to-be in a brand-new town. Someone needed to know who to call if she had a medical emergency.

And that someone should be me.

Cap's jaw clenched. He was just going to have to figure this out. A quick glance at the directory on the wall showed him that there were three different OB-GYN practices on the fourth floor. Minus any additional information, he was simply going to have to do this the Lovestruck way—by going door-to-door.

Thankfully, Cap was wearing his LFD shirt and cargo pants. Being a first responder in this type of delicate situation couldn't hurt. The receptionists he spoke with were surprisingly helpful. After the first two assured him that they didn't have any patients in the office by the name of Melanie Carlisle, he sprinted all the way to the third.

"Can I help you, sir?" A receptionist in pale blue scrubs decorated with cartoon storks looked up from her computer monitor and smiled.

God, I hope so. "I'm trying to find a patient— Melanie Carlisle? She had an appointment earlier this morning. We were supposed to meet in the lobby and I haven't heard from her. I'm starting to worry."

"Oh, I remember Melanie signing in earlier. Let me go check and see if she's still here." The receptionist stood. "You're her husband, I'm assuming?"

Apparently, the uniform could only get him so far.

"No, we're not actually…um." He held up a hand. "I'm not her husband."

"I understand. You're her partner," she said.

Cap didn't even hesitate. He didn't outright lie, but he smiled as if it were the truth.

"I'll be right back." She nodded, and then padded toward the back of the office in her baby blue athletic shoes.

Cap shifted from one foot to the other and glanced around the lobby. Only two women sat in the waiting area, which made his earlier assumption about the doctor being called away to deliver a baby seem unlikely. He'd managed to compartmentalize his panic while he'd been running all over the fourth floor, but now that he'd almost found her, it started rising to the surface. He felt like he was drowning in it, unable to think, unable to breathe.

He stared at the collage of baby photos on the waiting-room walls, but the faces of the newborns all seemed to blur together. Cap's heart should not have been beating so hard. Sweat shouldn't have been dripping down his back, between his shoulder blades. He'd dealt with countless medical emergencies in the course of his career. No one in the LFD could keep his calm like Cap could.

This was different, though. This was Melanie. She and her baby had to be okay. They *had* to.

But when the receptionist reappeared seconds later with a nurse in tow, he knew. It was written all over their faces.

"Captain McBride," the nurse said gently. "Melanie is having some trouble this morning. If you'll come with me, I'll take you to her."

Cap knew that tone of voice. He'd used it on countless occasions when he'd been forced to deliver bad news at the scenes of accidents, or sometimes even in hospitals, just like this one. He didn't like being on the receiving end of it, no matter how compassionate or serene it sounded.

He tried to respond but couldn't force a single word out of his mouth. So he just nodded and followed the nurse through a maze of hallways until they reached a door with a plaque on it that said Ultrasound Suite.

Cap remembered sitting beside his late wife and seeing an image of his unborn son for the first time in a room just like this one. It had been a day bursting with joy and hope. How things had changed since then. Lucy died of a sudden brain hemorrhage just six years later. Cap grieved…he moved on. But other than Eli, he'd never given his heart to another living soul again. He just hadn't had it in him.

But when the nurse pushed open the door and he caught sight of Melanie's tearstained face in the corner of the darkened room, the last remaining pieces of the wall around Cap's heart fell away. He'd torn down Melanie's wall with his own two hands, and somehow, while he wasn't looking, she'd torn down his in return.

"Cap?" Melanie glanced from him to the nurse and back again. "How…? What…? How are you here?"

"I'll give you two a minute. The doctor will back shortly," the nurse said, and then she left, shutting the door to the small room behind her with a soft click.

Melanie was sitting on the exam table, dressed in a hospital gown and wrapped in a fuzzy pink blanket, looking like a lost little lamb. So much about the heart-wrenching sight of her was wrong. Cap could hardly take it all in. His mind snagged on the strangest details as he tried to gather himself together. Whatever was happening, he wanted to be there for her. He *needed* to be there.

That blanket should be yellow. Yellow, like lemons.

"Cap," Melanie said again, bottom lip trembling. "I'm so glad you're here."

And all at a once, a steadfast calm came over him. He was at her side in a millisecond.

"It's okay." He stroked her hair. "Everything is going to be okay."

She buried her face into his shoulder. The poor thing was trembling from head to toe. She whispered against the crook of his neck, "They can't find the baby's heartbeat."

Cap's heart plummeted into a frightening free fall. He stroked her hair. "I'm here, darlin'. I'm right here."

She inhaled a shuddering breath. "The doctor said he'd come back and try again, but I'm scared. What happens if they still can't hear anything?"

Cap ran his hand over back in soothing circles. "Don't be scared. It's going to be okay."

Tears spilled down Melanie's cheeks, onto his LFD T-shirt. He hated seeing her like this. He knew she was scared. Terrified to her core. He wished he could come up with the right words to keep her fears at bay…to help her cling to the belief that everything would be just fine.

And then he realized he already knew the right words to say. He'd been listening to them each and every day. While he'd been concentrating on tuning out distractions and learning to focus on the tones and syllables coming from Melanie's lovely mouth, her message sank in. It was a part of him, and now—right when Melanie needed it most—he could give it back to her.

"Look at me, darlin'." He cupped her face in his hands. "Think about the lemons. Remember them? Spread out on the table, beneath the light of the spotlight? You wore that gold sequin gown, and you looked like a ray of light up there on that stage. And that's what you were. That's what you *are*—to me and so many other people."

Melanie blinked up at him through the hard glitter of tears.

Cap kept going. He didn't dare stop. "You make people believe in the good things, the happy things. And that's what you deserve, too—to believe."

She gave him a wobbly smile, and then he repeated her lemon speech back to her, word for word. The more he talked, the more Melanie seemed to calm down. Cap could feel her heartbeat pounding against his chest, and little by little, it grew slow. Steady.

When he finished, she took a deep breath and smiled. This time, the grin stayed put, even if it didn't quite reach her eyes.

"Wow," she whispered.

Cap didn't say anything. There wasn't a word he could utter that could compete with her own unbridled optimism, so he kissed the top of her head again and held her close to his chest.

The door swung open and the doctor entered the room.

"Let's try this again, shall we?" He looked up from the chart in his hands, gaze landing on Cap. "Oh, good, Daddy has arrived."

Daddy. As in, the father of Melanie's baby.

Perhaps Cap shouldn't have been so eager to let the doctor believe he was Melanie's "partner."

The misunderstanding didn't even seem to register with Melanie. She sat up and wiped the tears from her cheeks. "I'm ready."

The doctor smiled. "Okay, let's get you comfy."

Cap wasn't sure whether he should stay or leave and let Melanie have some privacy.

She grabbed his hand and squeezed it so hard that his fingers went numb. *Okay, got it. Stay.*

The few seconds that it took for the doctor to apply the ultrasound gel and get the fetal Doppler in place seemed to take a lifetime. And then, Cap's breath clogged in his throat as they waited, and waited, to hear something.

It was faint at first, and Cap thought maybe his tinnitus was acting up. Or perhaps the quiet thump-thump-thump was just a figment of his imagination, because he would have willed a noise to come from that machine if he could have. But then a lemon-bright smile splashed across Melanie's face as the sound of her baby's heartbeat filled the room.

Thump, thump, thump, thump, thump.

It was the most beautiful sound Cap had ever heard. If he never heard another thing as long he lived, he'd be just fine.

"There's your little one," the doctor said. "Your baby girl was just hiding from us earlier. Sometimes that happens."

They listened for a few more minutes, and then the doctor performed an ultrasound and confirmed what Melanie already knew—she was expecting a girl. Cap stayed for it all, and Melanie held on to him throughout, anchoring him in place.

Strangely enough, he didn't feel like an impostor. He was right where he was supposed to be. He felt it deep in his bones. After it was all over, Cap left the room so Melanie could get dressed. He waited for her back down in the lobby, just like always.

But this time, when she met him there, the first thing she did was wrap her arms around his neck, then gave him a long, deep kiss.

Until the roar in Cap's head didn't seem so important anymore.

Chapter Twelve

The following morning at Blush, Melanie unpacked a new shipment of exquisite baby and
toddler cotton dresses and shorts sets she'd or-
dered from England. Each piece had a smocked
section across the bib area that was embroi-
dered with dainty yellow ducks. Last week,
she'd bought every rubber ducky she could get
her hands on at Lovestruck's grocery store, The
Village Market, which she planned on using for
a big, interactive duck display, similar to her dinosaur setup.

Minutes before the boutique opened, she was

elbow-deep in squeaky yellow rubber ducks—hardly a situation that should prompt her to think about kissing Cap McBride, but alas, she couldn't seem to stop.

It was strange how intimate experiences tended to make you feel closer to a person. She'd been so frightened yesterday, terrified that her worst fear had come true and she'd lost the baby. And Cap had somehow swooped right in and held her hand through it all. Melanie wasn't sure what she would have done if he hadn't shown up. She'd been spiraling. It had been so unlike her, too. She was the lemonade queen, for goodness' sake. Thinking positive and looking on the bright side was her specialty. What had become of her?

Melanie fished her hand out of the box of ducks and rested her palm on her belly. The baby had been kicking up a storm this morning, and Melanie was grateful for every sensation, no matter how tiny.

This baby is important. She's not even here yet, and she's changed me. That's *what's become of me.*

But that wasn't all, was it? She'd kissed Cap, and it hadn't been a spontaneous, spur-of-the-moment thing. She'd been thinking about it for *days*, and yesterday, after he'd seen her at her most vulnerable and stuck by her side, she just hadn't been able to help herself. She'd thrown herself at him right there in the hospital lobby and kissed him as if there'd been no tomorrow.

And what a kiss it had been!

A shiver ran up and down her spine. It hadn't been a thank-you-for-attending-my-doctor's-appointment-and-pretending-to-be-my-baby's-father type kiss at all. It was more of a melt-into-a-puddle sort of kiss, complete with wobbly knees and a racing heartbeat. It had somehow seemed to last an eternity and just a split second, all at the same time. It was breathtaking, by far the best kiss she'd ever experienced.

But had it been real? Or had the closeness between them just been a product of heightened emotion? Melanie didn't know what to think. All she knew was that given the opportunity, she wanted to kiss Cap again. And again. And again.

As long as we both shall live...

Melanie gave such a violent start that rubber duckies jumped out of the box and scattered all over the floor. She couldn't possibly be thinking about *marrying* the man. They barely knew each other.

But pretending to be a family yesterday, even for just a short time, had felt so natural, so right. Was it possible that even though they didn't completely know one another, they knew enough about the things that mattered most of all? They fit together in a way that Melanie and Greg never had. She felt like herself around Cap—not the sparkly, beauty-queen version of herself that everyone knew and loved. He seemed to look past all of that and see the real her.

But she really doubted that Cap had any actual interest in her, romantically speaking. She was pregnant, which most men probably wouldn't find all that appealing in the dating department.

Then again, Cap wasn't most men.

"Good morning."

Melanie's head snapped in the direction of the shop door. She'd been so distracted by the memory of yesterday morning that she hadn't heard anyone step inside.

It was Cap—right there in the flesh—and he was holding an enormous bouquet of Vermont wildflowers and daffodils, as yellow and bright as the rubber duckies littering the floor at her feet.

"Cap, hi." Her face went warm. Good grief, she was a grown woman, a mother-to-be and she couldn't even look at him without blushing anymore.

"Hi, there." He held the flowers toward her. "These are for you. I just wanted to make sure you were okay. I know yesterday was rough."

Melanie took the bouquet and hugged it to her chest. It was like a flowery bundle of sunshine. "It was, but you made it better. Thank you again for being there. For me…and the baby."

"Anytime." He smiled, and then his expression turned thoughtful. Serious. "I mean that, you know. I want to be there for you—for you *and* the baby. You've both become very special to me. I want you to know that."

Joy blossomed inside Melanie, as bright and beautiful as the flowers in her arms. Her heart pounded so loud that she was afraid he might hear it. "I think the world of you, Cap."

They stood there for a tortuous second, gazing at one another as heat swirled between them—warmth, want and feelings that were far too intense to be pretend in any way. They weren't playing pretend anymore, and they both knew it.

A muscle in Cap's jaw flexed. His gaze dropped slowly to her lips, and then he stalked toward her with a gleam in his eyes that made Melanie tremble with anticipation. In a split second, his hands were buried in her hair and his mouth was on hers, worshipping...wanting. Melanie didn't feel at all like a washed-up beauty queen or geriatric pregnant person. She felt like a woman—seen, treasured, adored.

And then a loud squeak pierced the air, startling them both. Cap took a tiny backward step. *Squeak!* Then he took two more. *Squeak. Squeak.*

Melanie didn't want to spoil the romantic moment, but she couldn't help it. She collapsed into giggles. "It's the ducks."

Cap looked down. "So I see."

"I had a rubber-ducky avalanche before you arrived. Didn't you see them all over the floor when you walked in?"

"Oh, sweetheart," he said. "Don't you realize by now that I only have eyes for you?"

"Did anyone notice that there are rubber ducks in the shower stalls now?" Wade emerged from the locker room at the fire station with damp hair, a towel slung over his neck and a yellow rubber ducky in one of his hands.

He stood at the foot of the farm table in the kitchen and waited for Cap and Jack to look up from their respective sections of the *Lovestruck*

Bee. Cap had already pored over the local news section and moved on to the sports page, which had a good-sized article about the high-school lacrosse team. He needed to save it and take it home for Eli. Jack was busy reading Madison's fashion column, as per usual. Jack had been a reader of Madison's words since before they'd ever met in person. Of course, back then he claimed to only "hate-read" her column. Oh, how things had changed.

"Did either of you hear me?" Wade squeezed the duck. *Squeak, squeak, squeak.*

Jack finally looked up. "Where did that thing come from?"

Cap bit back a smile. "No idea."

Was it weird that he loved the sound those little ducks made now? Yes, probably best to keep that information to himself.

Wade pulled out a chair and sat down. "So, um, Cap. Something sort of weird happened last night while I was walking Duchess."

"What?" Jack snorted. "Duchess actually walked on her own four legs instead of forcing you to carry her around the block?"

Duchess, the elderly Cavalier King Charles Spaniel that Wade had inherited when his mom passed away, was famously spoiled. She had Wade wrapped around her furry little paw.

"Cute." Wade rolled his eyes. "But no."

"Madison swears up and down that she saw you pushing that dog in Nick's stroller the other day. I asked her if she snapped a picture and sadly, she did not," Jack said.

"Do you mind? I was talking to Cap."

Cap glanced at Wade over the top of his newspaper. "What is it?"

"I ran in to Charity Reed."

"The real-estate agent?" Jack asked.

Wade nodded. "Yeah, she was walking her chocolate Lab. He hit Duchess in the face with his wagging tail, and she was not happy. But I digress."

Cap and Wade exchanged an amused glance.

"Anyway, Charity knows Melanie. She's apparently the real-estate agent who sold Melanie her house," Wade said.

Cap shrugged. "Nothing weird about that. Charity is a real-estate agent. She probably sells houses every day."

"That wasn't the weird part." Wade shook his head. He frowned for a second, as if weighing how to proceed with the rest of the story.

"Spit it out, Ericson," Cap said.

"Well, Charity was up in Burlington yesterday visiting her mom in the hospital." Wade paused.

Cap leveled his gaze at Wade. He knew where this conversation was headed, and he honestly didn't care. Cap was in far too good of a mood to be bothered by small-town gossip. "Go on. Don't keep us in suspense."

"Okay." Wade shrugged. "She said she saw you and Melanie in the lobby together and that you two looked like—and I quote—'giddy new parents-to-be.'"

"Wait." Jack dragged his attention fully away from Madison's column. He cast Cap a sidelong glance. "Charity Reed thinks that you and Melanie are having a baby? *Together?*"

Wade nodded. "She definitely does."

Cap shrugged. "And?"

"And—" Wade sighed. "Well, there is no *and*. That's it."

"Fascinating story, Wade." Cap shook his head and grinned. "Riveting. Truly."

Jack stared at Cap. "What's happening? You seriously don't care that people are assuming you're the father of Melanie's baby?"

"That's exactly what I'm saying. I couldn't care less."

"You know if one person in Lovestruck thinks that, the whole town is sure to hear about it by sundown," Wade said.

"I'm not worried about it." Cap resumed reading the sports page. "If people are going to talk, let them talk."

"You're taking this awfully well," Wade said. "Much better than I expected."

"As far as rumors go, this one is pretty tame." Cap shrugged. Besides, nothing could spoil Cap's good humor today. Not a thing.

Wade dropped it, although Cap caught Wade and Jack studying him on occasion throughout the rest of their shift. Still, he didn't think much about it until later that evening, when he and Eli were eating dinner. Cap had made Eli's favorite—sloppy joes.

Eli didn't seem nearly as excited about the meal as Cap had anticipated. He picked a sesame seed off the top bun of his sandwich and nibbled on it.

"Something wrong?" Cap asked.

"I don't know." Eli sat back in his chair. "Why don't *you* tell me?"

Cap stopped chewing. Eli usually didn't dare speak to him with that tone of voice. "I beg your pardon?"

Eli sighed. "Is there something you want to tell me, Dad? I'm not a little kid anymore."

"I know you're not," Cap said. Eli was growing up before his very eyes. He'd gone through three different shoe sizes this school year alone.

"So then you know you can talk to me about things." Eli raised his eyebrows, clearly expecting Cap to share something important.

Ahh. Realization dawned as Cap remembered the conversation they'd had when Eli stopped by the firehouse to show off his good math grade. *This is about Melanie. Of course.*

"I suppose there is something I need to tell you," Cap said.

"Good." Eli practically sagged with relief. "Go ahead. Do it. Tell me."

"I have feelings for Melanie."

Eli just looked at him, completely unfazed.

"And I'm pretty sure she has feelings for me, too," Cap added.

"Okay," Eli said.

That was it? *Okay?* Cap would never understand teenagers. Teenagers and calculus—they were the two great mysteries of the universe. "For some reason, I thought you'd have more of an opinion on the matter."

"I do." Eli shrugged. "I like Melanie. I like

her a lot. I'm glad you two are…whatever you're doing. You need someone, Dad."

Cap studied his son. "You think so?"

His answer was unequivocal. "Yes."

"Okay, well, I'm glad you're on board with it. Your opinion means a lot to me. You know that."

Eli smiled and seemed to relax a little bit. He took a bite of his sloppy joe. "So there's nothing else?"

Cap laughed. "Isn't that enough for now?"

"I guess so," Eli said.

"I love you, kid. You know that, right?"

"Yes. You tell me all the time." Eli pulled a face.

And just like that, things felt normal again.

Melanie kept the daffodils that Cap had given her on the sales counter at Blush instead of taking them home. That way she could see them all day.

When she went back to the pink Victorian after a day on her feet at the boutique, Melanie was sometimes so tired that she fell into bed, and she couldn't very well look at them with her eyes closed. So the flowers stayed put, greeting her every morning with their sunny, butter-soft, yellow petals.

Three days after Cap had given them to her, they were still lush and alive, seeming to mirror how Melanie felt inside. She'd just returned to the boutique after closing up shop for a late lunch so she could have another picnic with Cap at the covered bridge and watch Eli's lacrosse practice, when a customer came into the shop to peruse the new rubber-ducky display.

"These dresses are just darling," she said.

"Thank you. They're new. I've only had them in for a few days." Melanie smiled. "They're from the UK."

"If I get one for my granddaughter and it doesn't fit, can I return it?"

"Absolutely." Melanie took the dress from the woman's hand and removed it from its dainty hanger. "Would you like me to gift-wrap it for you?"

"That would be lovely. Thank you." She pressed a hand to her chest. "I'm Nancy, by the way. I work at the *Bee* with your friend Madison. I'm the food columnist there. Madison just goes on and on about the beautiful things you have in stock. I figured I had to come check it out for myself."

Melanie arranged the tiny dress in a gift box,

tucking it between layers of blush-colored tissue paper. "I'm certainly glad you stopped by."

"Speaking of lovely." Nancy's face lit up as she examined the daffodils. "These flowers are stunning."

"Thanks so much. I think so."

"From Cap McBride, I assume?" Nancy shot Melanie a knowing smile.

That was strange. Just how well did Nancy know Madison? Melanie couldn't really imagine Madison oversharing about her love life with her coworkers at the *Bee*. Who knew, though? Maybe they were really close.

"Here you go." Melanie passed the gift-wrapped package across the counter to Nancy. "I hope your granddaughter loves it."

"Oh, I'm sure she will. Thank you, and congrats on your upcoming little one. It's so nice to see Cap happy again. Everyone in Lovestruck just loves him. He'll make a great father, you know." Nancy waved as she pushed the door open. "Toodle-oo."

"Wait," Melanie called after her. "He's not…"
The father.

She didn't bother finishing the thought out loud. Nancy was already gone.

Why on earth would she just assume that Cap

was the father of her baby? And why did this keep happening?

Probably because the two of you faked that you were in a relationship at the hospital.

But the hospital was miles away, in Burlington. Surely the Lovestruck rumor mill didn't reach that far and wide.

The shop door opened again, and the bells on the doorknob tinkled, announcing the arrival of another guest. This time, it was Madison.

Good. Melanie could get straight to the bottom of things before she drove herself crazy trying to figure out what was going on.

"Hey," Madison said. She gasped. "Oh. My. Gosh. The ducky dresses. I might have to do a write-up on them for my column."

She dug around in her Louis Vuitton tote and pulled out her cell phone. "Can I snap a few photos?"

"Of course, but first can I ask you something?"

Madison shrugged. "Sure, anything."

How to put this delicately? "Did you happen to say anything to Nancy at the *Bee* that would lead her to believe that Cap is the father of my baby? Accidentally, perhaps?"

"Absolutely not." Madison shook her head. "Not at all. That's just crazy pants."

"I know, right?" Melanie threw up her hands.

"I wouldn't worry about it, though. Nancy is totally harmless."

"Meaning, what? That she won't spread the rumor elsewhere?" Because it seemed like this particular nugget of #falsenews really needed to be contained.

Madison laughed. "Oh, no. She'll definitely talk about it, but in a nice way. A *complimentary* way. I meant she just won't print it in the paper."

Melanie stared at Madison, openmouthed.

"Nancy writes the food column," Madison said by way of explanation.

"I know," Melanie said. "She told me. I didn't even consider that she might write about it. I was kind of hoping she'd keep her erroneous assumptions about my baby's paternity to herself. Maybe I should say something to her."

"Oh, I wouldn't." Madison laughed. "That will only make it worse. Listen, it's really nothing to be concerned about. Small towns need things to talk about besides the maple syrup and what kind of cheese the wine bar is serving this week. I hate to say it, but you're the most interesting thing about Lovestruck right now."

Melanie felt her lips curve into a wan smile. "Lucky me."

"Oh, cheer up. It happens all the time. Last Christmas, everyone was convinced that Felicity and Wade were madly in love and planning to adopt a baby together when they were really just co–foster parents to Nick temporarily."

Melanie failed to see the logic in her argument. "But Felicity and Wade really are madly in love. And they adopted Nick together. They're an actual family. Literally everything you just said about them is true."

"But it wasn't back then. At least I don't think so…not entirely, anyway." Madison shrugged. "Feel better?"

For some reason, she didn't. Not quite.

"Maybe the rumor mill has a weird way of predicting the future. Now that would be a great story for the *Bee*." Madison waggled her eyebrows.

"I'm not sure I'll ever get used to this town," Melanie said.

But a girl could try.

Chapter Thirteen

The following morning, Cap gave Eli a ride to school on the way to the firehouse.

Cap had always liked stolen moments like this one. Because his shift started so early in the morning, Eli usually walked to school an hour or so after Cap had left the house. But this week marked the start of two-a-day lacrosse practices at school. The state playoffs began in just a few weeks, and Lovestruck High was poised to make it all the way to the final tournament in Montpelier. So, early in the predawn hours, Eli piled his lacrosse gear and his school backpack into the back of Cap's truck and they headed down Main Street toward the old country road that led to the high school.

Call him crazy, but Cap was feeling celebratory. While Eli had been in the shower, Cap had made buttermilk biscuit kolacky—a bona fide hot breakfast. The sausage was maple-flavored and the can of biscuits he'd used contained a dash of golden honey, so the end result was as Lovestruck as anything Cap could have grabbed for them at The Bean. He'd picked up a thing or two from Jack in the kitchen over the last few years.

"Have one," he said, passing a foil-wrapped kolacky to Eli as the truck crawled down Main Street.

A crowd of power-walking Lovestruck moms was already gathered outside The Bean, each holding a latte in one hand and pushing a baby stroller with the other. The women all seemed to stare directly at Cap as he drove past. He gave them a finger wave and kept on going.

Eli sat quietly beside him, the foil packet in his hand untouched.

"Aren't you going to eat that?" Cap said.

Eli shrugged. "Not right now. Maybe later."

Cap studied him. "You love kolacky, and

you've got a tough day ahead—practice before and after school. You should probably eat something, son."

"The booster club is having their lacrosse pancake breakfast this morning."

"I see." Cap's kolacky had been beat out by the allure of fluffy pancakes and homegrown Vermont maple syrup. No surprise there. "Maybe you can save it for lunch, then?"

Eli nodded silently and slouched farther down in his seat.

Cap felt himself frown. Being a teenager, Eli didn't typically chat Cap's ear off. Sometimes he seemed more interested in his phone than what was going on in the world around him. That was normal, though, so Cap tried not to give him a hard time about it.

But something about Eli's demeanor this morning seemed off—even more off than at their sloppy joe dinner two nights ago. Cap snuck a glance at him as they approached the turnoff for Old Country Road. "Everything going okay with calculus?"

"Yes. I got a B-plus on the quiz we had yesterday." Eli's tone was flat. Just a little while ago, a good grade on a calculus quiz had been such a jubilant occasion that it had warranted a surprise visit to the fire station.

Eli had never been much of a morning person, but Cap couldn't help wondering if his son was somehow out of sorts. "Melanie offered to come over and help you again whenever you're having trouble."

Silence.

Cap's irritation flared, but he was already turning into the high-school parking lot. "Eli? You're sure everything is okay at school?"

"It's fine, Dad. I promise," Eli reached for the door handle. "I have to get to practice now."

Cap patted his son on the shoulder. "Okay, you have a good day now."

"I will." Eli shot him a sheepish grin. "Thanks for the ride. And the kolacky."

"No problem. Love you, son."

Eli rolled his eyes and got out of the car. Cap had breached the universal, unspoken rule—No Parental Affection While on School Property—because, of course he had. It's what dads did.

Some things never changed.

With only two days left to go until the children's pageant, Blush Boutique was suddenly the busiest place in town.

Melanie's store was wall-to-wall strollers within minutes of opening up shop. The parents of kids who were participating in the pageant had apparently all decided that new, crown-worthy outfits were in order, and descended on Blush directly after morning coffee at The Bean.

"Oh, my gosh, what's happening here?" Felicity's eyes went wide as she stopped by the boutique after her early-morning yoga class. Nick was strapped to her chest in a BabyBjörn carrier, with his chubby little legs dangling beneath him. "I've never seen your store so busy."

Melanie grinned. "I think everyone is just excited about the pageant."

"I told you it would be a hit," Felicity said. Then she glanced toward the dinosaur display and gasped. "Uh-oh, you didn't let someone else buy the cute T. rex shorts set, did you? That's what Nick is planning on wearing."

Nick babbled away in his carrier, oblivious to any impending infant fashion disasters.

"Nick will be adorable, no matter what he wears. I promise," Melanie said.

"Obviously. He's the sweetest baby in Lovestruck." Felicity let Nick grab her pointer finger and then pressed a gentle kiss to the back of his tiny hand. "But what will the judges think if another baby shows up in the same outfit?"

Melanie arched an eyebrow. "Aren't you forgetting something? There *are* no judges. It's not that kind of a pageant, remember?"

Every child who entered would get a crown, because the point wasn't to compete. It was to have a good time and learn a little bit about community service and confidence. For the tinier kids, like Nick, the pageant was a family-bonding event. No judging required.

"Oh, right. I keep forgetting. I think the sashes and rhinestones must be going to my head." Felicity pulled a face.

Melanie glanced around her packed store. "You're not alone. I think the whole town has gone crown crazy."

"Listen, I've been thinking…"

Melanie redirected her attention back to Felicity, who definitely looked like she had something up her sleeve. "And?"

"Since the clothing drive was a joint project between the fire department and the pageant, maybe someone from the LFD should have an official role on the big day." Felicity cast a meaningful look at the firehouse across the street.

Melanie took a deep breath. She didn't disagree with the idea…in theory. She'd actually considered the same thing. Maybe the LFD could park a fire truck in the town square, right next to the gazebo. They could give lessons to the kids on fire safety between different parts of the pageant.

Only two things were holding her back.

Felicity frowned. "You're not still upset about the lemon-bar incident, are you?"

And behold, Thing One.

"No, of course not." Melanie shook her head. How could she possibly hold a grudge about that? So much had changed since that day, mainly her feelings about Cap. Still, she didn't want to put him on the spot.

But her biggest concern by far didn't have anything to do with lemon bars…

"Then what's stopping you?" Felicity said.

Melanie glanced down at her baby bump and back up at her friend. "You realize that people are seriously starting to think that Cap is the father, right?"

It was Melanie's fault. She'd gone ahead and let everyone at her doctor's office believe that Cap was the daddy. She had no idea who at the hospital had been the actual source of the rumor, but failing to correct that assumption probably hadn't been helpful.

"News flash—he doesn't seem to mind much." Felicity arched an eyebrow. "You do realize he's completely crazy about you, don't you?"

Joy warmed Melanie from within. Rumors aside, she'd hardly stopped smiling since returning from the last trip to Burlington. "I'm beginning to think so, yes."

"And you clearly feel the same way, so I'm not understanding the problem here," Felicity said. Nick shifted in his carrier, so she started bouncing on her toes and rubbing a soothing hand on his back.

"I don't know. It's just complicated. He has a son, and I'm pregnant. And having him cohost a pageant with me doesn't seem like the best idea when whatever is happening between us is all anyone can talk about. I can't just let everyone assume he's the baby's father. It doesn't feel right."

"What are you going to do, rent a billboard and splash 'hashtag fake news' across it?" Felicity said.

Not a bad idea.

Melanie sighed. "Of course not. I'm just saying that asking Cap to cohost the pageant is not to going to happen. Period."

"Okay, but if you decide you want a firefighter up there in the gazebo with you, just let me know. I'm sure Wade would be happy to do it."

"I'll keep that in mind." Right now, Melanie was half-afraid to be seen even talking to any of the men in Lovestruck. Who knew what sort of crazy theory would pop up next?

Nick squirmed and let loose with another stream of baby talk. Felicity bounced with renewed vigor. "I need to get him home. When I saw how packed it was in here, I just wanted to come check on you. Do you need any help with anything? No one wants you to overdo it, you know."

Melanie rested a hand on her belly. "Thanks, but I'm fine. I promise. My new assistant manager is taking over at lunchtime and I'm going to go home and put my feet up for a bit. All is well. Besides, helping pick out pageant clothes is one of my favorite things in the world." She flashed a wink. "Even when they've got dinosaurs marching across them instead of sequins."

The rest of the morning passed in a blur. By the time Melanie turned things over to Ruby, her new employee, it seemed as if every person walking along Main Street had a shopping bag from Blush Boutique dangling from their arm.

Melanie felt light on her feet, like she could float all the way back to her pretty pink Victorian. It was happening—she was making a name for herself in Lovestruck. A *place* for her and her baby-to-be. A true home.

All day long, customers had addressed her by name, as if she'd been operating the children's shop for years. Two different people had invited her to join the baby-bootee-knitting class at Alice's yarn shop. One of the moms she always saw power walking with the ladies outside The Bean had even brought her a platter of homemade sugar-maple candy, fashioned into delicate maple leaves. It was a delicacy that Melanie had never heard of before, but after just a nibble, she was already a fan. A big one.

She lingered on the sidewalk to take a look at the boutique's display windows. Miraculously, they were still presentable, even after the frenzy of prepageant shopping.

"Oh, hi, Melanie. I'm so glad I caught you."

Melanie's gaze darted to the reflection beside hers in the window, and she froze.

Diane Foster was standing just behind her.

"You're not closing up shop already, are you?" Diane's red lips curved into a pout.

Why now? Melanie was in such a great mood. The last person she wanted to talk to was Diane Foster. That billboard idea was sounding better by the minute.

Melanie took a deep breath and turned to face her. "No, we're open. I'm heading home, though. I'm sure Ruby can help you if you have some shopping to do."

Melanie smiled at the sleeping child inside Diane's stroller. "Bye-bye, little one. See you at the pageant."

Before she could take a step, Diane stopped her. "Actually, I came to see *you*. Not shop."

"Great," Melanie said, as if having a conversation with Diane Foster were the next best thing to world peace. "*So* great. What can I do for you?"

She shot a glance over toward the fire station. *Help! 911!*

But her telepathic call for assistance was in no way effective. Jack, Wade and Brody were engaged in a heated game of H-O-R-S-E at the basketball hoop affixed to the side wall of the apparatus bay, oblivious to Melanie's suffering. Cap was nowhere to be seen.

"I just wanted to apologize for my behavior a while back," Diane said.

Melanie narrowed her eyes at the woman, waiting for the other shoe to drop.

"You know, for asking about the baby's father," she said in mock whisper loud enough for everyone within a square mile of Main Street to hear.

"It's fine," Melanie said, even though it definitely wasn't fine. Never had been, never would be. She just wanted to move on before Diane had a chance to come out and say something about Cap being the father.

Honestly, did people really believe that nonsense? She'd clearly been pregnant when she first arrived in town. Where did they think Cap had been hiding her for the first five months of pregnancy?

"No, really. I feel bad about it. I never would have asked if I'd known…" Diane let her voice drift off as if they were both in on a shared, salacious secret.

Then, something snapped inside Melanie. Lovestruck was her home now—as much her home as it was Diane Foster's. She couldn't keep trying to avoid the small-town rumor mill, hoping the gossips would just move on to something else. It was time to set the record straight, once and for all.

She squared her shoulders and looked Diane straight in the eyes. "Diane, Cap McBride is not the father of my baby."

Diane didn't appear fazed in the slightest. "Of course, he isn't."

"Oh." Melanie crossed her arms and promptly uncrossed them. If the unspoken secret that Diane had been hinting at didn't have anything to do with Cap, then what exactly was she referring to?

"What I'm trying to say is that I never would have asked about the baby's father if I'd know you'd gone to a—" Diane leaned closer and lowered her voice "—sperm bank."

Melanie went numb. A terrible, icy sensation pricked its way down her spine.

Her hands flew to her stomach, like she could somehow protect her unborn child from hearing what a tiny baby couldn't possibly understand.

She wanted to scream. *No!* This was her personal, private information—hers to tell when the time was right. How was it possible that she was hearing it tossed about on Main Street by Diane Foster, of all people?

"Um…" Melanie finally said.

She felt sick all of a sudden, like she might throw up right there on the sidewalk in plain view of the entirety of Lovestruck, despite never having experienced a single episode of morning sickness.

"Not that there's anything wrong with it." Diane waved a hand. "Of course, there's not. I just never would have asked about a human father when there isn't one."

She frowned to herself, as if she were trying to figure out one of Eli's differential equations. "I suppose there is, though. Somewhere out there. But you know what I mean."

Bile rose up the back of Melanie's throat, but she swallowed it down. She hadn't breathed a word about her baby's paternity to anyone. Not even her doctor in Burlington knew the truth—just her doctor back in Texas. All she wanted was a new start in a new town, with a life she built for herself on her own terms. She'd only dared to share the truth with one person, because she'd been convinced she was falling in love…that she could trust him.

Cap.

A terrible knot lodged in her throat. So hard and thick that Melanie could barely swallow around it.

"I do," Melanie said. "I know exactly what you mean."

He had done this. The man who'd held her hand and let her cry all over him when her world had been falling apart. The man who'd whispered to her about lemons and love and life, and convinced her that everything would be just fine. The man who'd almost made her believe in picket fences again.

Melanie didn't want to believe it, but how could she not? It was the only logical explanation.

Diane kept talking, and Melanie was only vaguely aware of the woman's voice droning in the background. Every bit of her attention was focused on the firehouse across the street. And then, as if she'd somehow conjured him, there was Cap—smiling at her as he walked from the building to the apparatus bay…waving as if everything was just fine and dandy.

And that's what did it. That's when Melanie Carlisle, the brightest, sunniest, *happiest* Miss America to ever rock a tiara, finally lost her beauty-queen composure.

Chapter Fourteen

Cap wasn't sure what made him take a glance out of his office window around lunchtime. Maybe on some instinctual level, he'd known Melanie would be standing outside on the sidewalk. Or maybe he'd fallen so head over heels in love with her that he looked out the window dozens of times a day in hopes of catching a glimpse of her.

Probably the latter.

Things had been moving at warp speed around Lovestruck since their return from Burlington. Melanie's pregnancy scare had convinced her that she needed to hire someone to help out at Blush sooner, rather than later. After a flurry of interviews, she'd found a college graduate who'd worked as an au pair overseas. With the lacrosse finals right around the corner, Cap had attended an unusually high number of practices and playoff games.

And then there was the children's pageant. The pageant, more than anything else, had dominated every facet of daily life in Lovestruck. The other firefighters in the department had been showing him pictures of their kids in an attempt to get Cap to weigh in on everything from outfits to smiles to posture. Cap was at a loss. Did toddlers even have posture?

He was ready for the entire thing to be over with. As soon as Melanie was finished crowning every child in a fifty-mile radius, Cap was going to tell her how felt about her. He didn't want to detract from the occasion because she'd poured a lot of effort into it, so he was biding his time. For now.

But in two days, all bets were off. He was going to tell her he loved her and that he wanted to build a life with her, her baby and Eli. The second she'd kissed him, he'd become a goner. Just call him Mr. America.

A flicker of worry passed through him when he realized the person chatting with Melanie was Diane Foster. Melanie hadn't said so specifically, but he would have bet money that Diane had been the one who'd asked Melanie about her baby's paternity on the day of their picnic at the covered bridge.

Diane wasn't necessarily a bad person, but she definitely had a tendency to poke her nose in everyone else's business. In classic Diane fashion, she usually felt bad about it afterward. But sometimes, an apology was too little, too late. Cap had a feeling now might be one of those times.

He pushed away from his desk and headed outside. He'd simply walk over there and extricate Melanie from the conversation, if necessary. He didn't like the idea of Diane asking questions about Melanie's baby, not when it had upset her so much last time.

A basketball flew past his head and went into the net with swish as he exited the apparatus bay. Wade high-fived himself.

"Want to join us, Cap?" Jack called.

Cap held up a hand. "Not now. I'm going across the street for a few minutes. I'll be back shortly."

He squinted toward Blush, where Melanie

suddenly wrapped her arms around herself. One of her hands flew to her throat.

Cap's gut churned. What was going on over there?

Melanie's gaze darted toward him and he waved, but the second she set eyes on him, her face crumpled.

Cap froze in place for a second. Then adrenaline coursed through him fast and hard, the same way it did when the fire alarm sounded at the station. He ran toward her to see what was wrong.

Diane kept talking, oblivious to both Melanie's distress and Cap's presence. But then Melanie walked away from her, gaze trained on Cap. She barely even glanced both ways before she started marching across the street, leaving a frowning Diane Foster in her wake.

"Darlin', what's wrong?" Cap reached for her to guide her toward the curb. Lovestruck was as small town as they came, but they were in the middle of Main Street, the busiest thoroughfare in town.

Melanie stared daggers at him. "Don't touch me. Do. Not."

Cap stumbled to a halt. What had he missed? He hadn't seen Melanie this visibly upset since her doctor wasn't able to find her baby's heartbeat in the ultrasound room. The memory of Melanie's tearstained face that morning would be seared into Cap's consciousness for as long as he lived. That look had been different, though. That look had been pure devastation. Loss, grief…heartbreak at its very worst. Seeing her like that had made Cap ache in the deepest part of his soul.

That raw ache was back now. One look at Melanie's red-rimmed eyes and anyone would have been able to tell she was heartbroken again, but this time there was an edge to it. She wasn't just devastated.

She was *furious*.

At him, apparently.

"What have you done?" she said quietly, so low that he could barely hear her above the constant roar in his ears, no matter how hard he concentrated on the shapes her lovely mouth was making as she spoke. Then she repeated herself—louder, so there was no mistaking the anguish in her tone. *"What have you done?"*

Cap held up his hands like he would if he was approaching a wounded deer. "Melanie, you're going to have to give me a hint here, darlin'. I have no idea why you're so upset."

"Diane *knows*." Melanie waved her arms to encompass the general vicinity of Main Street, which had come to a complete standstill. "And now everyone else probably knows, too."

"Well, hon. I didn't know it was a secret," Diane called from the sidewalk.

Cap cut his gaze toward her, and she immediately began steering her baby stroller in the opposite direction. Cars were beginning to line up on either side of where Cap and Melanie stood. The crowd clustered around the entrance to The Bean was watching with rapt interest.

"Who did you tell?" Melanie demanded.

Cap shook his head. He still didn't know what he'd supposedly said or done…

And then it all snapped into place in his mind with sickening finality. Only one thing in the world would make Melanie this upset. The secret she'd told him echoed in his head, drowning out everything else.

I went to a sperm bank. That's why I don't like it when people ask about the baby's father. It's personal, between my baby and me. Someday I'll tell my child all about it. The last thing I'd want is for her to hear it from someone else.

"I didn't tell a soul." Cap shook his head.

"Honey, I'd never betray your confidence like that."

"Well, Diane knows, and I know for a fact that I didn't tell her." Melanie's voice broke, and something inside Cap broke along with it. "Just you. You're the only person in Lovestruck I've opened up to about it."

This couldn't be happening. There had to be some sort of explanation. Cap hadn't breathed a word about the circumstances surrounding Melanie's pregnancy to anyone. He knew how close she held her child's privacy to her heart. He wanted to build a life with her. A family.

There had to be another explanation.

"Melanie, let's get out of the street. Come with me and we'll figure this out. I promise." Cap acknowledged the paused motorists with a nod.

"No," Melanie said. Her tone had gone from enraged to eerily calm on a dime.

Oddly enough, Cap preferred enraged. The sudden coldness in her voice made him feel leaden.

He took a tentative step toward her, and when she backed away from him, a weight settled on his heart.

"We can't stay here, honey. It's not safe," he said.

"I've got this. It's fine," someone said. It was

Wade, who jogged past them and began to divert traffic down the closest side street.

Then Jack appeared at Cap's side. "Everything okay over here? Is there anything I can do?"

Cap's jaw clenched. "We're fine."

They had to be. Cap didn't know how, but he'd find a way to make sense of this terrible mistake.

"Melanie?" Jack turned kind eyes on her. "How about we get you out of the street?"

"I want to go home," she said. "Not the firehouse. *Home*."

Jack nodded. "Of course. I can make that happen."

He was handling the situation exactly as he should, as opposed to Cap, who'd been unable to help in the slightest.

The weight on his heart felt too heavy to bear. *She doesn't trust you anymore.*

"Alice?" Jack waved Alice Jules over from the curb.

She shimmied past Cap and wrapped one of the hand-knit blankets her yarn shop was so famous for around Melanie's slender shoulders.

Was there a single person in Lovestruck who wasn't going to hear that Cap McBride had broken Miss America's heart in the middle of Main Street?

Probably not, but Cap didn't care. He just wanted to get to the bottom of this. He wanted to fix it, but it was beginning to seem like the situation might not be fixable.

"Come on, dear." Alice took Melanie by the hand, and Melanie let the older woman and Jack escort her off the street.

Jack shot him a sympathetic look as they walked past him. So did Alice, but Melanie kept her head down. She wouldn't even look at him anymore.

Cap knew better than to follow.

"I don't understand." Madison shook her head. "This doesn't make sense at all. I just can't see Cap talking about something so important behind your back."

Melanie warmed her hands on the mug of lavender lemon tea that Alice had just handed her and glanced around at her surroundings.

She was in Alice's knitting shop, surrounded by yarn—so *very much* yarn. Skeins and balls of it were tucked into cubbyholes that lined the walls on all four sides. Fuzzy yarn, bulky yarn and dainty, delicate yarn in every possible shade imaginable. It was like being inside a box of crayons.

Alice's dog, Toby, a hairless, lovable little thing who looked more like a Dr. Seuss character than an actual canine, was curled into a tiny ball in Melanie's lap. Melanie might just stay right where she was for the rest of her life. It sure seemed like a better idea than showing her face out on the public streets of Lovestruck again.

"Tell me I didn't just literally stop traffic to confront him in the street," Melanie said.

She'd just made things so much worse, hadn't she? If the entire town hadn't already been talking about her baby's paternity, they were *definitely* talking about it now. And Diane and Cap weren't entirely to blame. This time, she'd done it to herself.

"You kind of did, honey." Felicity winced. "But you had every right to be upset. Plus, you're pregnant."

Indeed she was. Who knew that her decision to have a baby all on her own would become such a newsworthy event?

"Alice, I feel bad that you closed your shop. I can go," Melanie said, but she couldn't seem to move a muscle. She was beyond tired, both physically and emotionally.

When Jack had interrupted her argument with Cap, all she'd wanted to do was lock herself in her little pink Victorian and hide. But Alice had swept Melanie straight into Main Street Yarn, flipped the sign on the door to Closed and called for reinforcements.

Melanie couldn't deny that being surrounded by her closest Lovestruck friends, a hairless dog and more yarn than she'd ever seen in her life had made her feel better. Her heart still felt like it had been through a paper shredder, but she wasn't completely alone. The little life she'd built in Lovestruck was still standing strong. It was just missing her favorite piece.

Cap.

She sipped her tea and tried to force his handsome face from her mind. *Permanently.* It wouldn't be hard to live in a small town without ever having to set eyes on the fire captain, would it?

"I'll hear of no such thing," Alice said, patting Melanie's leg as she sat down beside her. "You'll stay right here with us until you feel better. The shop can wait. As far as I know, Lovestruck doesn't have any impending yarn emergencies."

Alice winked at her, and Melanie gave her a weak grin. Apparently, she hadn't completely lost her ability to smile. What an unexpected surprise.

"I'm sorry, hon, but I have to agree with Madison. Cap is like a father to Wade. I can't imagine him doing something like this." Felicity looked up from a tangle of yarn she was attempting to knit into something remotely resembling a baby sock. "Are you absolutely sure you didn't tell anyone else?"

Melanie had been asking herself the same question over and over again, but every time, she came back to the same answer. "I'm positive."

Madison arched one of her perfectly groomed eyebrows. "You don't think it was your ex, do you? The guy you dated back in Dallas?"

After she and Felicity had arrived at the yarn shop, Melanie had filled them all in on the breakup, the sperm bank…all of it. Why not? Her life was an open book now, apparently. And it wasn't quite as glittery and perfect as it looked from the outside.

But once she'd opened up about everything, Melanie had finally been able to breathe again.

"Maybe Greg is somewhere in Lovestruck right now, trying to win you back," Felicity said.

Madison tilted her head. "And he ran in to Diane Foster…"

"I just don't see how any of that is remotely possible," Melanie said.

"So once again, we're back to Cap being the culprit." Madison sighed.

"I'll admit he hasn't really been himself lately," Felicity said. "But it still seems unlike him to do something like this."

Melanie knew exactly why Cap had been out of sorts lately, but she wasn't about to utter a word about his auditory therapy or his tinnitus. Just because he'd betrayed her confidence didn't mean she was going to betray his.

"Why do I feel like we've had this exact conversation before?" Madison's forehead crinkled.

"Because we have." Felicity stabbed at her tangle of yarn with a knitting needle. "Just a few weeks ago when Melanie overheard him saying some unflattering things about the pageant."

"Oh, my gosh, the pageant." Melanie blinked. "It's the day after tomorrow. I almost forgot."

"Everything for the pageant is under control, dear. People are so looking forward to it." Alice smiled. "Don't you worry about a thing."

Madison nodded. "It's going to go off without a hitch. We've got your back."

"And the best thing about small towns is that as soon as something big happens, everyone forgets about whatever they were all talking about and they move on to the next thing." Felicity grinned. "Like crowns."

"Take our word for it," Madison said. "No one is going to be talking about sperm banks once the pageant is in full swing."

Felicity looked up from her knitting. "They'll probably forget all about you and Cap shutting down Main Street, too."

But would Melanie?

Cap somehow made it through the rest of the day at work. In effort to keep his mind off things, he went out on calls and let Brody stay behind at the station to handle dispatch.

Cap accompanied Jack and Wade out to a car fire on the interstate. From there, they had a few medical calls and at the end of their shift came the most dreaded emergency of all: Fancy the cat.

"She's stuck in the tree again?" Wade said. "How is that even possible?"

Jack didn't say a word—he was probably hoping to blend into the woodwork and avoid being assigned to go rescue Lovestruck's least favorite feline.

"I'll go," Cap said.

Brody, Wade and Jack all stared at him, mouths agape.

"Are you serious?" Wade said.

"Yep." Cap headed toward the apparatus bay for his turnout gear. He needed more protective gear to face that Persian than he would if he'd been headed to a four-alarm fire.

Brody crossed his arms. "But why? You have seniority."

"You never go out on Fancy calls," Jack said. "Not that I blame you. If I had seniority, I wouldn't do them, either. It's the main reason I want your job one day."

"The main reason?" Cap arched an eyebrow. "I thought it was the only reason."

"Ouch." Brody laughed.

See? Cap could do this. He could go about his regular life and joke around with the guys at the station. He could mix things up and rescue cats in trees. His entire life wasn't over just because Melanie Carlisle had decided he was some kind of monster.

Never mind that volunteering to go save Fancy was a penance. If anyone deserved to be shredded by a cat today, it was Cap. He should have found a way to get Melanie out of the street and somewhere private so they could talk. He'd been so stunned by the entire turn of events that he hadn't been able to think straight. He still couldn't, really. That's why he'd been in action mode all day. If he just kept moving, he could get through the day in one piece. Once he got home, he might finally let himself think about how spectacularly everything had fallen apart.

Wade had other ideas, though. "I'll come along."

"Seriously?" Brody said. "You're volunteering, too?"

Jack shook his head. "Don't question it. Just let them go."

Fancy was in a bad mood, as always. Cap wondered if there was such a thing as anger-management groups for animals. If not, there should be. Then again, maybe the reason Fancy was never happy to see anyone from the LFD was because every time they stopped by, she was in the embarrassing position of being stuck in a sugar-maple tree.

In any event, Fancy still wasn't the angriest female he'd come across today. Just the first runner-up.

"Do you want to talk about it?" Wade said once they were inside the red LFD truck and on their way back to the firehouse.

Cap kept his gaze the road, grip tightening on the steering wheel. "About the cat rescue? I think it went as well as could be expected. We're both still in one piece, and neither of us ended up in an ambulance—which is more than Jack was able to say last year."

"I'm not talking about the cat rescue." Wade's gaze slid toward Cap.

He probably should have seen this coming when Wade volunteered to come along. Cap and Wade had been through a lot together, especially last Christmas, when Wade had decided to adopt Nick. The fact that Wade wanted to check in and make sure Cap was okay shouldn't have come as a surprise in the slightest.

Cap's throat went thick, all the same. "I'd really prefer not discuss it."

Wade ignored him and kept on discussing it, anyway. Wasn't that how families always seemed to work? "She was upset, Cap. If you say you didn't betray her confidence, I believe you. You know that. You're the most upstanding person I know. Just give her some time to cool off, and try talking to her again when the dust has settled."

Cap shook his head. "I don't think so."

"Look, I know you can be set in your ways about things…"

Seriously? Cap shot him a glare.

"Relax, I'm not calling you old. I'm just saying that you're used to running things around the department and being the guy everyone depends on, the guy everyone respects. Having your character come into question can't be easy." Wade's left eyebrow shot up. "Especially for you."

It wasn't. Not at all. Just like it wasn't easy trying to imagine giving up his role with the LFD or losing his career because of his medical diagnosis. Why did it feel like so much of Cap's life was hanging by a thread?

"You care about her," Wade said, his tone going soft. "I've known you a long time, Cap McBride, and I think this is the first time I've ever seen you in love."

Cap shook his head. "That's not what this is."

He'd thought so…maybe. Okay, definitely.

But how could it be love if Melanie believed that he would tell random citizens of Lovestruck, or anyone else, for that matter, intimate secrets about her pregnancy? Things looked bad. Cap knew they did, but he couldn't get past the fact that nothing he said or did could convince Melanie that he was innocent. He'd never hurt her like that. If she believed that he could, maybe what they had wasn't really love at all. They'd experienced some intense emotional moments together in the short time they'd known each other. Maybe he'd simply mistaken it for more than it really was.

"With all due respect, Cap." Wade shook his head. "A man doesn't grovel in the middle of Main Street for anything but true love."

Cap shifted in the driver's seat. Point taken. "If she doesn't believe me, I'm not sure what I could possibly say to convince her otherwise."

"So, what? You're just going to give up and not even try?" Wade said as Cap guided the truck onto Main Street.

Cap's chest tightened. This was officially his least favorite street in all of Lovestruck now. Too bad the firehouse was located smack in the middle of it.

The truck rolled to a stop in the apparatus bay, and Wade sighed. "Are you going to answer me? What are you going to do?"

Cap let his head fall back on the headrest. He was so tired all of a sudden that he could barely keep his eyes open. "I have no idea."

Wade climbed out of the truck, but Cap stayed put. He just needed a few minutes to gather himself before heading inside the firehouse. How was it possible that it was only four o'clock in the afternoon and he was still on duty? Cap felt like he'd lived a lifetime in a single day.

He took a few deep breaths. In any other circumstance, he would have reached for his phone and done one of his focus exercises. He couldn't bring himself to watch Melanie's lemonade video, though. Not now—maybe not ever.

So he dragged himself out of the truck and slammed the door shut behind him. The other firefighters were in the corner of the apparatus bay that served as a gym, working out with the weight sets as Wade gave them a play-by-play of the Fancy rescue. Cap strode straight to his office without a word.

And when he got there, he found someone waiting for him.

"Eli?" Cap looked his son up and down for any visible signs of injury. Why wasn't he at practice? "What are you doing here? Are you okay?"

Eli sat slumped in the big leather chair behind Cap's desk. Gone was the confident teenager who'd so recently waved a calculus test under Cap's nose in this very spot. In his place sat a wide-eyed kid—a kid who clearly needed his dad.

"I'm not hurt," he said quietly.

Cap clicked the door to his office closed, and studied Eli's frowning face. Something definitely wasn't right with this picture. "I don't understand. Why aren't you at lacrosse practice?"

"Because I messed up, and I needed to come talk to you right away."

"Okay." Cap nodded. A mistake was better than something more serious, like a concussion or a broken bone, both of which were things that Cap worried about every time Eli picked up a lacrosse stick. A mistake could be fixed, and at least his son had come to him about it instead of letting Cap find out from the principal. "Is it calculus again?"

Eli shook his head. "No."

Cap crossed his arms and tried his best to be patient, but it was tall order on today of all days. "Son, help me out here. I can't help you if you don't tell me what the problem is."

"It was me," Eli said quietly. Then he looked up and finally met Cap's gaze. "I'm sorry, Dad. I only told Sam from the team this morning at the pancake breakfast because he kept saying you were the father. Then Sam told someone else, and Mrs. Foster was there volunteering. And after school, everyone was saying that Melanie had been crying in the street."

Dread settled in Cap's chest with a terrible ache. Eli was talking a mile a minute, but Cap's mind kept snagging on bits and pieces—*he kept saying you were the father, and Mrs. Foster was there volunteering, Melanie crying in the street.*

It couldn't be, though. Eli didn't know anything about Melanie's pregnancy. He couldn't have been the one who'd told her secret. But the look on Eli's face told a different story.

"Oh, son…no."

Chapter Fifteen

Cap couldn't breathe. It took all of his concentration to simply take in oxygen and let it out again.

Eli had been the one who'd spilled the beans? Melanie's very, very *personal* beans? How was that even possible?

Cap sank into the chair opposite Eli, who was still sitting behind Cap's desk looking like a schoolkid who was visiting the firehouse on a field trip.

"Eli." Cap counted to five in his head so he wouldn't lose his temper. "I need you to start again from the beginning. What you shared with Sam was private information. How did you even know about it?"

"I heard you and Melanie talking about it that night when she came over to help me with calculus," Eli said in a small voice.

Cap gritted his teeth. What else had he and Melanie talked about during that conversation? He wasn't entirely sure. What stood out to him most was that they'd almost kissed...*would have* kissed, if Eli hadn't interrupted them asking about pizza.

"So you spied on our private discussion?" he said.

Eli nodded, and if Cap wasn't mistaken there was a hint of defiance in his eyes instead of remorse.

Cap regarded him through narrowed eyes. "That's not really like you, son."

Eli's face went red. "I had to. I kept asking you what was going on and you weren't telling me the truth."

Cap sat back in his chair as if he'd been slapped. "What? When you first asked me if Melanie and I were dating and I said no, I was telling the truth. As soon as I knew things were changing, I talked to you about it. You told me you liked her. I got the impression that you were happy that I'd found someone I enjoyed spending time with."

It was more than that, though, wasn't it? He didn't just enjoy spending time with Melanie. He wanted *forever* with her. There was a reason that Cap hadn't dated since he'd lost Lucy. He wasn't the type of person who had casual relationships. He'd been holding out for the real deal. He just hadn't realized until now.

Eli's forehead scrunched. "I do like Melanie."

"Then again, I don't understand the problem."

"It's you, Dad. I wasn't worried about Melanie. I was worried about you." Eli threw up his hands, and his face went three shades redder. "You've got that weird machine by your bed. You've been acting weird for weeks, and you're going to the hospital up in Burlington all the time. Every week it's a new excuse. I'm not dumb, Dad. I knew you were going up there at the same time every week. I thought something terrible was wrong with you, like what happened to Mom. I thought you might be dying, Dad, and you were afraid to tell me. So, yeah, I listened, and I'm not sorry."

Then the bottom fell out of Cap's stomach. Eli thought he'd been *dying*?

"It's nothing like that." Cap shook his head. Why had he tried to keep the truth about his hearing a secret? He and Eli talked about everything.

Correction: everything but *this*. Cap had let his stupid pride get in the way of communicating with his own family, and look what a mess he'd created.

"I'm not dying. I'm just having some trouble with my hearing." Cap closed his eyes for a beat. *Tell him the rest. Now isn't the time to hold back.* "I'll probably need to get hearing aids. I've been stressed about how that might affect my work, but I should have been more open about it…with you and with the guys here at the station. I'm sorry."

"I know," Eli said.

Of course, he did. He'd overheard everything.

"But I'm glad you finally decided to tell me. Dad, no one cares if you have to wear hearing aids. Everyone loves you. They'll help you adjust. I will, too."

And just like that, Eli was back to sounding like a mini-adult. Except none of this explained why he'd wreaked havoc today by spreading news that wasn't his to spread.

"I should have talked to you, and I understand

why you were upset that I didn't, but that doesn't excuse what you did today," Cap said.

What in the world was he going to do? He'd claimed innocence and denied everything, but somehow his worst nightmare had come true. He *was* at fault…at least a little bit. Eli was his son, his responsibility. How was he going to tell Melanie about this?

"Everyone's been saying you're the father," Eli said flatly.

"That's just gossip and you know it."

"I know. But everyone at school was saying it was the truth and you were lying to me." Eli shook his head. "I just sort of snapped."

Because I've been lying to you about something else for weeks. A lie by omission was still a lie, after all.

"When I told Sam about Melanie, I wasn't thinking about how it would affect her. I swear. I guess I was still mad at you, and I had no idea it would turn into such a big deal. You have to believe me." A tear slipped down his cheek, and Cap almost felt like crying himself. He hadn't seen Eli shed a tear since Lucy's funeral. After he'd lost his mom, Eli had hidden behind a veil of stoicism. Like father, like son. "I never meant to hurt Melanie."

Cap nodded. Eli had meant to lash out at him, and the woman Cap cared about—the woman he *loved*—had gotten caught in the crosshairs.

"What happens now?" Eli said, gnawing on his bottom lip.

They hadn't even touched on the fact that Eli had bolted from school, missing afternoon play-offs practice and probably a myriad other things. The consequences from today would reach far and wide—including being grounded, at minimum.

First and foremost, though, Cap was worried about Melanie. She was the damaged party here, and he didn't have the first clue how to make it up to her. Her entire plan for how to tell her child about where she had come from and how she'd been conceived was completely blown out of the water now. It didn't get any more serious than that.

"I don't know, son." Cap dropped his head in his hands. "I just don't know."

Melanie stayed at the yarn store until late afternoon. Once she'd washed her face in Alice's bathroom and stopped by Blush to make sure her new employee had everything under control, Madison and Felicity walked her home.

Once she was settled in the pink Victorian—with the blanket that Alice had insisted she keep—Melanie practically had to force her friends to leave. Madison and Felicity were worried about her, but Melanie assured them she'd be fine on her own. They both had husbands and kids. She couldn't keep letting them babysit her. Her heart had been broken, but she wasn't incapacitated.

Melanie had a pageant to put on in just two days. She had a business to run and a baby's room to decorate. She couldn't wallow.

By 5:00 p.m., she'd already taken a warm bath, climbed into her favorite maternity pajamas and nestled into Alice's blanket on the sofa with a book. After the day she'd had, an evening of self-care was in order. She'd hit the ground running tomorrow.

Melanie didn't dare turn on the television in case she and Cap made the evening news. This was Lovestruck, after all. She buried her face in the pages of her book, but before she could read a full sentence, the letters blurred together behind a veil of tears.

How could she have been so wrong about Cap?

Had she been wrong about him? He'd seemed genuinely shocked when she confronted him.

And so insistent. Every time she closed her eyes, she remembered the anguished look on his face…the urgency in his tone.

I didn't tell a soul. Honey, I'd never betray your confidence like that.

If Cap hadn't done it, who had?

The doorbell rang, and it startled Melanie so bad that she nearly jumped off the sofa. She didn't want to see anyone, especially not tonight. The way things were going, she wouldn't have been surprised if Diane Foster had dropped by with another soul-crushing pseudoapology.

Whoever was on the other side of the door wasn't going to take no for an answer, apparently. The doorbell rang two more times in rapid succession.

Melanie scrambled off the couch. She was being silly. She couldn't barricade herself in her house forever. It was probably just Felicity or Madison stopping by to check on her. Maybe even Alice.

"Who is it?" she called.

"It's me," Cap said from the other side of the door. "Eli is with me."

Melanie stared at the door and didn't move a muscle. If Cap had been alone, she might have thought he'd come by to apologize. But he wouldn't have brought Eli along for that.

Surely, this didn't have anything to do with math.

"Can we come in for a minute? It's important." Cap sounded as weary as Melanie felt. More so, if such a thing was possible. "Please?"

It was the *please* that wore her down. Cap's voice hitched when he'd said, breaking the word into two syllables. Melanie's heart felt like it was tearing right along with it.

"Please tell me this isn't a calculus emergency," Melanie said as she opened the door.

Cap met her gaze, and the pain she saw in his eyes seemed to burrow deep in her chest. Eli stood beside him with red-rimmed eyes. They looked so forlorn that it frightened her.

Melanie wasn't ready to see Cap. Not yet. Just the sight of him confused her. She didn't know whether she wanted to kiss him or tell him how badly he'd hurt her, and the fact that she couldn't decide rattled her.

"Come in." She opened the door wider, and wrapped her arms around herself as they stepped inside her cozy living room.

Just hold it together. You can fall apart after they leave.

Cap glanced at Eli and then back at Melanie. "Thanks for letting us in. I know this is a bad time and I should have at least called first, but…"

His voice trailed off, and the air between them swirled with all the things left unsaid.

Melanie swallowed hard. "It's okay."

"No, it's really not." Cap shook his head. "Eli has something he wants to say."

Melanie glanced at Cap's son, and in the instant before he said anything, she knew. Every ounce of color had drained from his face, and he kept his gaze glued to the floor. There was only one possible reason why Eli would be almost unable to look her in the face.

"Dad wasn't the one who told people about your baby. It was me." Eli inhaled a ragged breath. "I'm sorry. Please don't be mad at my dad anymore."

Cap shot her an apologetic glance. "I didn't know he was going to say that last part. Sorry. You can be as mad at me as you like."

Melanie didn't know if she was still angry with Cap or not. She felt like she was experiencing every possible emotion at once. Relief and regret warred inside of her, and on top of it all, she was just plain shocked.

It had been Eli. Melanie just couldn't wrap her head around it, much less her heart.

"I didn't realize it was going to be such a big deal, but I still shouldn't have said anything. I wish I could take it back." Eli's eyes went shiny with unshed tears. "I would if I could."

Melanie nodded. She stopped short of telling him it was okay, because it wasn't. Still, she couldn't help but feel a tiny bit sorry for him. He'd obviously had no idea what sort of mess he'd put in motion.

"We're friends, aren't we, Eli?" Melanie asked.

He nodded, finally meeting her gaze. "Yes."

"Then why? I don't understand."

"I was mad at Dad. Some of the kids started saying he was the father, and everything kind of spiraled from there." Eli shot Cap a pleading look.

"I've told you how I feel about Melanie, son. We talked about this."

Melanie held up a hand. "You know what? I think we've all been through enough today. I'm tired, and it's getting late…"

Right. It wasn't even six o'clock. Even pregnant women didn't fall into bed that early.

Cap's gaze swiveled toward Eli. "Son, can

you please go wait in the car? I need to talk to Melanie for a minute in private before we go."

"Yes, sir." Eli gave Melanie a sad smile. "Good night. I really am sorry."

"I know you are, Eli. I'm glad you came to tell me."

It couldn't have been easy. The poor kid looked as upset as Melanie felt. "Good night."

Her heart twisted as she watched him go. Eli was a good kid. He'd done a stupid thing, but at least he'd owned up to it. Melanie had worked with teenagers long enough in her pageant-coaching business to know that they sometimes made choices without thinking them through. It was part of being a kid, part of growing up.

But Eli wasn't the only one who was going to have to live with the consequences of this particular mistake. Melanie would, too. So would her baby.

None of them would get out of this unaffected.

The door clicked shut behind Eli, and as Cap drew closer to her, the pull Melanie felt toward him was almost impossible to resist. She couldn't just let herself fall into his arms again, though. As much as she wanted to move on and pretend that none of the past twenty-four hours had happened, it wouldn't be the right thing to do—not for anyone.

Melanie took a tiny backward step, and Cap let his outstretched arms fall to his sides. She braced herself for another apology, but what he said next nearly brought her to her knees.

"This wasn't how I wanted to do this, but I need to tell you now—I'm in love with you, Mel. I know everything's a mess, but what matters most is how we feel about each other. I love you." His mouth twisted into a smile, at long last. "I can't seem to stop saying it. I love you. I want us to be a family—all four of us. Don't give up on me, darlin'. Don't give up on *us*."

Melanie had waited her entire life for someone to say such words to her. She'd just always imagined she'd be in a much happier state when she finally heard them.

She bit down hard on her lip to keep from crying. She felt like she'd shed enough tears in the past few days to last a lifetime. The thought of getting through the next few days in Lovestruck was overwhelming. Melanie couldn't quite picture her life beyond the pageant. "I don't know what to say."

He guided her face upward with a gentle brush of his fingertips, until their eyes met. His velvety brown irises shone with promises—promises she wasn't sure she knew how to believe in anymore.

"Say yes," he whispered.

And it was so tempting, but try as she might, she couldn't seem to force the word out of her mouth.

Everything Greg had said to her during their breakup kept spinning through her mind. Maybe she really wasn't cut out for a family. Cap and Eli had been just fine until she'd come along. Cap should probably go check on his picket fence. It had probably spontaneously combusted at some point this afternoon.

Maybe Melanie was better off alone. She still had to figure out how to be a mom. How could she have possibly thought she could properly love someone at the same time?

"I'm sorry." She pressed her fingertips to her trembling lips. Why couldn't she say it? "I just can't."

Cap's ears roared. Maybe he'd misheard. *Please... Please let me have misheard.*

But Melanie didn't look like a woman who'd just accepted a pseudomarriage proposal. If Cap wasn't mistaken, there was a trace of pity in her sorrowful green eyes. She felt sorry for him…

because he'd just laid his heart on the line and she was turning him down.

He couldn't blame his tinnitus or hearing loss on this one. Melanie's denial was loud and clear.

"Oh," he said.

Smooth. Real smooth.

"It's not that I don't feel the same way." She swallowed, and Cap traced the movement up and down her slender throat. "But we can't, Cap. Everything's gotten far too complicated. What happened to today with Eli—"

"Eli adores you. What he did was inexcusable, and I take full responsibility for it. I should have been honest with him about my diagnosis, but instead I wanted to protect him. If I'd talked to him like I should have, he never would have listened to our conversation that night." If only Cap could go back in time and do things right…

But he couldn't. All he could do was try to take whatever they had left and make something beautiful of it. Something *real*. Something that would last forever.

Lemons to lemonade.

"I'm not sure Eli is ready for me to become part of your family, Cap, and I would never want to come between you and your son. In fact—"

She took a deep, shuddering breath. "Eli is probably right."

Cap narrowed his gaze at her. "Right about what?"

She waved a hand back and forth between them. "Right that you and I don't belong together."

"Eli never said that, nor does he think it." Cap's heart pounded hard in his chest. This botched proposal was going from bad to worse. He should have done this right—down on one knee, with a ring in his hand—instead of turning up on Melanie's doorstep at the end of a day like this one.

But Cap had felt her slipping away, and he'd been desperate to stop it. Desperate to hang on to what they had. For once in his life, he'd acted impulsively and he'd made things exponentially worse—at least he thought he had. He still didn't know the first thing about exponentials or differential equations.

But as little as he knew about math, Cap definitely understood that he and Melanie were somehow greater than the sum of their parts. He'd known it since the moment she'd found him in the hardware store, questioning the meaning of his life.

Cap had found his meaning now, and it was all because of Melanie. He'd been an idiot to try and handle his diagnosis on his own. Wade and Jack had shown up for him earlier today, and they'd do it again. Every time he needed them. Eli, too. Cap just had to work on getting better at realizing he couldn't control everything and asking for help when he needed it. What had happened today was wake-up call.

But Cap couldn't let it come between him and Melanie. He *wouldn't*.

You and I don't belong together.

Had Melanie really just said that?

Well, Cap definitely couldn't control this particular situation. He needed all the help in the world and he wasn't afraid to admit it. "Melanie, don't do this, please. I know you don't believe that."

She shook her head. Her eyes were almost wild...wide with fear. "It was crazy to think this could work. Look at me."

She waved a hand at her midsection.

Cap couldn't help but smile, despite the panic coursing through his veins. "I *am* looking at you, sweetheart."

She was the most beautiful woman in the world. And she was *his*. But neither of those things were what she needed to hear at the moment. "And you're going to be a great mother."

This was about the things her ex had said to her before she moved to Lovestruck. It had to be. How could a man spend nearly a decade loving this woman and not have any idea who she really was or what she held most dear in the world? Cap couldn't begin to understand it.

Because he didn't love her the way that you do. Not the real *her.*

Melanie deserved a real relationship, the kind she wanted on her terms. And Cap's deepest desire was to give it to her.

But he couldn't do it alone. Not if she wouldn't let him.

"I'm sorry," she whispered, and then she turned around, walked into her bedroom and closed the door, shutting Cap out for good.

Chapter Sixteen

Melanie somehow got through the following thirty-six hours on autopilot. She threw herself into the frenzy of pageant preparations and tried to make her mind a complete blank. As long as she kept herself busy and kept moving, it worked. Move, move, move. That was the solution—bury the heartbreak. Don't let herself think about it.

Just.

Keep.

Going.

"Who wrapped the gazebo in the town square

in twinkle lights?" Madison asked as she stood at the Blush sales counter gently packing a box full of tiny, kid-sized crowns in bubble wrap.

Melanie had pulled in every favor she could within the pageant world to get the custom-designed crowns in on time. She'd sketched a simple design with a rhinestone *L*—for Lovestruck—in the center, along with a glittery little bumblebee floating through the gemstones, since the *Lovestruck Bee* had agreed to sponsor the pageant. The paper had arranged for ice-cream and cupcake trucks to park in the town square for the afternoon with free sweets for everyone in attendance. Plus they'd covered the rental fee for the rows upon rows of white folding chairs that Melanie set up in front of the gazebo during Lovestruck's predawn hours, and they'd scheduled a child-friendly deejay to play songs from animated Disney movies. Melanie had also arranged for a few party princesses and superhero characters to join in on the fun—a last-minute addition that had required her to spend hours on the phone when she should have been sleeping. But while she'd been trying to lure Cinderella and Batman to Lovestruck, she hadn't thought about Cap once.

Okay, maybe she'd thought about him once.

Or twice. Five times, tops. But it had certainly been fewer times than if she'd been lying in bed instead of trying to turn Lovestruck's town square into its own little theme park for the pageant.

"The gazebo is covered in twinkle lights?" Felicity looked up from her clipboard, which contained the checklist they'd all been poring over since the pageant committee convened at Blush at nine o'clock this morning. Alice and the knitting crew had taken over babysitting duties, keeping an eye on Nick, Emma and Ella at Main Street Yarn while Felicity, Madison and Melanie worked pageant logistics. The festivities were scheduled to start soon. Just two hours and counting. "Twinkle lights aren't on this list."

"I did," Melanie said. "I thought it would be nice addition. Wait until you see it. I used twenty strands, ten thousand lights in all. It looks magical."

Felicity and Madison exchanged a glance.

"When on earth did you have time to wrap the gazebo in ten thousand twinkle lights?" Madison said.

"Late last night," Melanie said. It wasn't as if she could do it during the day. She was doing her best to avoid Main Street during the daylight hours, lest she see Cap milling about the firehouse. She couldn't avoid him forever, obviously. But she wasn't ready to see him yet. Her heart just couldn't take it.

I can't seem to stop saying it. I love you. I want us to be a family—all four of us. Don't give up on me, darlin'. Don't give up on us.

Melanie shook her head in an effort to rattle the words from her brain, but they kept spinning around, over and over again, like a favorite song on repeat.

"Late last night," Felicity echoed, eyes narrowing. "Before or after you rounded up your character posse?"

"Before."

"But neither of those things are on the list." Madison's gaze turned sympathetic. "Hon, are you getting any sleep at all?"

"I'm fine, just busy trying to give the kids of Lovestruck the best day possible." Melanie's smile went wobbly, so she looked down at the pageant schedule in front of her, going over the minute-by-minute agenda for the tenth time.

Felicity rested a hand on Melanie's forearm, forcing her to meet her gaze. "We just want to make sure you're taking care of yourself, Mel. The last few days have been a lot."

Melanie swallowed. *Don't make me talk about it. Please.* If she had to relive her visit from Cap and Eli the night before last, she'd fall to pieces. That could wait until after the pageant. It had to.

"Are you sure you don't want to talk about it?" Madison asked.

Melanie nodded "I'm positive."

Felicity gave her a sad smile. "If it makes you feel any better, Wade says that Cap is a mess. He really misses you."

It didn't make her feel better. *Nothing* did. "Can we please just get back to the pageant preparations? We still have a lot to do before this evening."

"Like hire a skywriter? Or organize a parade?" Madison winked.

Melanie had actually considered a parade, but thought it best not to mention it.

Felicity glanced at the time on her phone. "Right now, according to our schedule, we should load everything up and take it down to the town square to get set up. The fire department should have blocked all road traffic half an hour ago. Pedestrians only down there until after the pageant."

"The fire department?" A flare of panic went off in Melanie's chest. If she never saw another fire truck again, it would be too soon. But she supposed this was what she got for putting a firefighter's wife in charge of traffic control.

Madison nodded. "They did a lot of work on Crowns and Coats. We had to include them, don't you think?"

"Of course." Melanie's hands shook as she snapped the lid onto a plastic bin full of pageant sashes.

How had she let herself forget that the LFD would have a presence at the pageant? Surely, Cap, Lovestruck's least-favorite fan of children's pageants, wouldn't show up. He had to know that she needed some space. Plus she had a feeling he didn't want to see her any more than she wanted to see him. He hadn't called or texted once since she'd turned down his impromptu proposal.

Not that she'd *wanted* him to call or text, because she didn't. The only reason she kept checking her phone was to make sure it remained blessedly notification-free.

Keep telling yourself that, lemonade queen.

"Okay, then. Let's get this stuff down to the town square." Melanie picked up the box of sashes. It was quite a bit heavier than she'd expected, probably because she'd chosen sashes with a bedazzled trim.

She swayed a bit.

"Whoa, let me help you with that." Madison plucked the bin from Melanie's arms.

"It's fine." Melanie held on to the counter to steady herself. She glanced at the dinosaur display and the T. rex went fuzzy around the edges. "I'm fine."

Maybe if she said it enough times, she could make it be true.

Something caught her eye beyond her plastic prehistoric friends—a flash of red out the boutique's front window. Melanie made the mistake of taking a proper look. The fire truck was parked in front of the firehouse like it always was, and as per usual, it was being washed by hand. Cap had once told her that fire trucks all over the country were washed every single morning. It was a firefighting tradition, apparently.

Jack, Wade and Brody weren't doing the sudsy work themselves this morning, though. Instead, Eli was going over the truck with a wet, soapy sponge while Cap pointed at different parts of the enormous vehicle, issuing instructions.

Melanie rested her hand on heart. This must have been part of Eli's penance. She wasn't sure why the sight of him washing that big truck all by himself made her feel so unspeakably sad all of a sudden. Or why seeing Cap stirred up a longing inside of her that was too strong and too deep to ignore, no matter how much busy work she created for herself.

Don't lie to yourself. You know exactly why.

She loved him. She loved them both. She just didn't know how to take these particular lemons and turn them into lemonade. It felt impossible.

"Mel, are you sure you're okay? You look a little pale," Felicity said.

Her voice sounded weird, like she was talking to Melanie from the end of a very long, very dark tunnel. The dinosaurs went blurrier, until Melanie couldn't tell the T. rex from the stegosaurus, which was ridiculous because they had very little in common. One of them was a carnivore, while the other was a herbivore. Everyone knew that.

And then everything tilted sideways and Melanie's whole world went black.

Cap squinted into the sunshine, shielding his eyes as Eli went over the shiny red surface of the fire truck with a sponge. Eli was grounded, of course. Cap didn't want to leave him home alone on a Saturday, lest he get any ideas about venturing beyond the confines of the house, although Cap doubted he would. Eli seemed sincerely contrite. Still, since Cap had to work all day at the station, he'd brought Eli along and put him to work.

First up, Eli had been assigned to wash the fire truck. Afterward, he'd be cleaning the firehouse bathrooms until it was time for him to head to Saturday afternoon lacrosse practice, the only activity he was allowed to attend outside of school. Saturday practice wasn't an official, school-mandated exercise, but since Eli had missed an official practice last week, Cap thought he owed it to his team members to show up. Until then, he was at the LFD's beck and call.

"Looking good, Eli," Wade said as he came to stand beside Cap in the driveway.

Eli waved his sponge in reply and gave Wade a half smile.

Eli hadn't been doing much smiling over the last few days, but then again, neither had Cap. He kept hoping he'd hear from Melanie, kept thinking that if he wished hard enough, he'd be able to squeeze lemons into lemonade by desire alone. So far, his glass was bone-dry.

Cap had picked up the phone a million times to text or call her since their sad goodbye the other night. But he didn't want to pressure her or make things worse than they already were. She knew where he stood. The only thing he could do now was wait.

And wait some more.

Cap had never been good at that sort of thing, but he was learning, determined to do better. Determined to start fresh and let go of his need to control every possible outcome when things in his world went topsy-turvy.

"I got everyone together like you asked," Wade said, angling his gaze toward Cap. "They're all waiting for you around the farm table."

"All right, then." Cap forced a smile. "Here goes nothing."

He strode back into the firehouse with Wade following a step or two behind him. Like Wade said, the others were sitting around the station's big farm table in the kitchen—Jack and Brody, plus all the firefighters from the A and B shifts, too.

Department-wide meetings that included all three shifts at one time were rare. Cap couldn't remember the last time he'd called everyone in at once. But this wouldn't take long, and it was important. He'd been putting if off for far too much time.

Wade took a seat beside Jack, but Cap remained standing.

"Hello, everyone. Sorry to drag you in on a Saturday if you weren't scheduled to work today. I promise I'll be quick. I wanted to tell you all at once so everyone would hear the news from me instead of finding out via the Lovestruck rumor mill," Cap said. He'd had enough of the gossip circuit to last a lifetime.

The men all exchanged looks. Not one of them cracked a joke or a smile. They clearly knew that whatever Cap had to say was serious.

"A few weeks ago, I was diagnosed with NIHL, noise-induced hearing loss, accompanied by tinnitus. Some of you have probably heard of the condition before. It can be an occupational hazard for anyone who works around loud noises, firefighters included."

No one said a word as they waited for Cap to continue, but he could see the concern in their eyes. Not just that, but affection, too.

He focused on the wood grain of the table so he could just get through the rest of his speech and get it over with. "As you know communication is critical in firefighting. I've been undergoing auditory therapy up in Burlington and it's been helping but not enough. So I've decided to give hearing aids a try. Hopefully, they'll be successful enough that I can keep serving as your captain."

He took a deep breath. "Anyway, I just wanted to personally let everyone know what was going on. That's it."

There, he'd said it. He'd admitted he wasn't perfect and that he didn't know what might happen next. Cap had never felt more vulnerable in his life, but he'd done it.

Wade was the first to stand and wrap him a big bear hug. "It's going to be fine. You could have told us sooner, you know? We're family."

Jack hugged him next. "I have twin toddlers at home. I don't have the energy to take over your job yet." He winked. "We'll make it work. You're not going anywhere."

And so it went. Somehow Cap got through the parade of well-wishes dry-eyed. The message was a unified one—no one was ready for Cap to leave. They were committed to helping Cap deal with the situation and finding a way to stay on. For the first time in months, Cap felt like he could breathe.

And then Wade's and Jack's phones both starting ringing at the same time.

Wade glanced at the display screen on his cell. "It's Felicity."

"And Madison." Jack frowned down at his phone.

Both of them calling at once didn't seem like a coincidence. Weren't they supposed to be with Melanie, helping get ready for the pageant?

Alarm bells went off in Cap's mind, clearer and louder than any of the ringing in his ears.

"Go ahead and take it. We're finished here," he said.

Eli walked into the room as most of the fire-fighters were filing out.

"I might need another sponge, Dad," he said. "That's a very big truck."

Cap chuckled, but the smile died on his lips as he caught Wade's and Jack's ends of the conversations with their wives.

"Is she still unconscious?"

"Don't move her. We'll be right there."

They hung up at the same time and both stared at Cap with twin expressions of concern.

He knew what was coming next. After days and weeks and months of yearning to hear things as crisply and clearly as possible, in that moment, Cap wanted nothing more than silence. He desperately didn't want to hear whatever they were about to say.

"I'm sorry," Wade said. "But it's Melanie."

Chapter Seventeen

When Melanie's eyes fluttered open, it seemed
as if half the citizens of Lovestruck were
crammed inside her sweet little boutique. Felicity and Madison were there, just as she remembered, except now they were peering at her
intently.

For the life of her, she couldn't remember
Wade, Jack and the mystery man with a stetho-
scope hanging around his neck having been
there a few minutes ago. And she was *certain*
that Cap and Eli weren't supposed to be there…
yet there they stood, just feet away.

The ache in Cap's eyes was palpable. His soft brown irises looked almost black, and a knot of muscle flexed in his jaw. Melanie wasn't sure she'd ever seen Cap appear so intensely worried—not even in the ultrasound room at the hospital, or the other night when she'd been doing her best to push him away. She had the strangest urge to run her fingertips along the rugged planes of his face and caress away his worry lines. Followed by a tender kiss, for good measure.

That didn't seem appropriate, considering he'd all but handed her his heart on a silver platter and she'd refused him. So Melanie dragged her gaze away and focused on Eli instead. But Cap's son was looking at her with such concern in his young face that it made Melanie want to scramble to her feet and go give him a hug.

Wait a minute. Why *was* everyone looking at her like that? And what was she doing lying flat on her back on the boutique floor?

Melanie tried to sit up, but she could barely move. She felt like she'd been shot with a tranquilizer gun—the gigantic kind they used on zoo animals.

"Whoa there," Doctor White Coat said. "Take it easy, Melanie. You fainted. You need to rest right there for a few minutes before you try and sit up, okay?"

"Okay," she obediently replied. At the moment, being upright seemed exceedingly overrated.

She *fainted*? Well, this was new. Melanie had never fainted before—*ever*. Not even in the torturous seconds when she'd been standing on the Miss America stage, waiting to hear if she would be crowned the winner or the first runner-up.

She frowned at the doctor. "Who are you, again?"

"I'm Dr. Dan." He grinned. Melanie noticed that the necktie he was wearing had googly eyes and a red-felt forked tongue protruding from the neat point at the bottom of it, so that the tie looked like a snake. That seemed odd. Was fainting always this disorienting? "We haven't formally met yet."

"Dr. Dan is the pediatrician in town." Felicity waved a hand in the direction of Main Street. "His office is right around the corner."

Well, that explained the serpent tie.

"I'm the only local physician on call today. I'll be your baby's doctor after she's born." Dr. Dan smiled again. It was the sort of smile that seemed like it could soothe colicky babies and small children with tonsillitis.

But Melanie was neither of those things, and now that she was getting her wits about herself, she was beginning to think that maybe it wasn't such a great thing that she was a heavily pregnant woman who'd just fainted.

"Is there something wrong with my baby? Why did I faint?" She tried to sit up again.

This time, Cap swooped down to cradle her head in his lap. It felt so good to touch him again that Melanie nearly wept.

"You and the baby are just fine," Cap whispered and flashed her a wink.

Melanie nodded. Everything was going to be okay…and Cap didn't hate her, apparently. That was a relief.

"Your heart rate seems a bit elevated, and your blood pressure is low," Dr. Dan said. "You're suffering from mild dehydration."

Dehydration? That seemed about right. Melanie had cried buckets the past few days.

"When was the time you ate or drank something?" The doctor arched an eyebrow.

"Not recently, I'm sure," Madison said.

Felicity nodded. "She's been working really

hard the past day or so. She's putting on the children's pageant in just a couple of hours."

Dr. Dan shook his head. "Not anymore, she's not."

Melanie's eyes drifted closed. Cap was stroking her hair, and it felt so good that she just wanted to take a nap, right there on the floor— a preplanned nap, this time. Not a spontaneous, loss-of-consciousness sort of nap.

But then she realized what Dr. Dan had just said. "What? Yes, I am. I've been working on this pageant for weeks."

"Sorry, but no. What you need is at least twenty-four hours of bed rest and plenty of fluids. Popsicles, ice chips, Sprite…those sort of things. You absolutely should not be participating in that grand spectacular that seems to be going down in the town square today." Dr. Dan shot her a sympathetic look. "You really can't be too careful with a—"

God help her, if Dr. Dan said the words *geriatric pregnancy*, she was going to strangle him with his gaudy snake tie.

"I understand," she blurted. "I'll do it. We'll just have to cancel the pageant."

All that work. Ugh. The children were going to be so disappointed, but Melanie had to think about her baby girl first. In her grief and confusion, she clearly hadn't been taking good enough care of herself. Her body wasn't just hers anymore. It belonged to her daughter, too, and nothing was as important as bringing that precious girl into the world as healthy as she possibly could.

"What? No." Felicity shook her head. "We'll just have to do it without out you. It's too late to cancel now."

"I think you're right. The ice-cream and cupcake trucks are already parked, the gazebo and chairs are set up and I'm pretty sure I saw Batman and Cinderella milling around down there," Madison said.

Jack's eyebrows drew together. "I'm not even going to ask."

"It's best you don't," Madison said. "As we said, Melanie might have gone a little overboard in the past couple of days."

Cap's eyes met hers. He knew precisely what she'd been up to.

Just.

Keep.

Going.

Had she really thought she could outrun heartbreak?

"Who's going to be the emcee? I'm not sure I know enough about pageants to take the helm." Felicity sighed.

"Oh!" Eli stepped into view. "Dad does."

"Um," Cap said.

Eli shrugged. "What? You do. I've seen you watching that YouTube video from that super old pageant a bunch of times."

"It's not *that* old," Cap and Melanie said simultaneously.

Their eyes met again and laughter bubbled up Melanie's throat. Then Cap's gaze turned tender and he bent his head down and kissed her as gently as if she were made of glass.

His lips were warm and soft and reverent, and familiar in a way that made Melanie remember all the reasons she'd fallen so hard for him to begin with. How had she lost sight of all those stolen moments, all the unexpected ways he'd made her feel like she belonged here in Lovestruck? Like she belonged with *him*.

He pulled back, just a little bit, and the grin on Cap's face was enough to wipe the dreaded lemon-bar incident from Melanie's memory for good…among other painful things.

"I'll do it," he said. "I'll run the pageant in Melanie's place."

* * *

Cap introduced toddlers in tutus, he held a microphone to the ground as five-year-olds tap-danced, he placed a bedazzled crown onto the delicate head of every child in Lovestruck—plus a few kiddos from other parts of Vermont who'd traveled to their charming town for the occasion. And he did it all with a smile so big and infectious that Melanie could feel it all the way from her snuggly brass bed in the pink Victorian cottage that no longer felt like a house, but a home.

Eli videoed the entire affair, and the *Bee* live-streamed it on the newspaper's official social-media channels, so Melanie didn't miss a single second of the pageant. Her friends had gotten her all set up in her bedroom before heading to the town square. Melanie was covered with the blanket that Alice had given her, her pillows were fluffed, she had water, Jell-O and chicken soup, all just an arm's length away. And lemonade, too—Cap had made it from scratch from her backyard lemons. He'd apparently learned quite a bit from her old Miss America talent routine and fully grasped the concept of turning lemons into lemonade on a literal level, as well as a metaphorical one.

Melanie still wasn't quite sure where she and

Cap stood. They hadn't had time to figure that out before the pageant, nor had they had a single second of alone time together. But she knew what she wanted, and she was no longer afraid to reach out and take it if the opportunity presented itself again.

Life wasn't a pageant. There weren't neatly defined events that she could prepare for, like the interview portion or the talent competition. Melanie had arrived in Lovestruck with a plan, but Vermont wasn't a stage and her place here wasn't as easily categorized as the age divisions in the pageant system. It wasn't until she let her beauty-queen smile slip that she realized that it was okay to let go. How many times had she told her students that a dropped baton or a missed note in a musical solo wasn't the end of the world? Sometimes the most beautiful things in life were the most unexpected, like being crowned Miss America when there were only ten days left of the reign. Or discovering you had a lemon tree in your backyard. Or stumbling upon the love of your life in a mom-and-pop hardware store on your first day in a brand-new town.

Melanie had always been a little bit of an outsider in the pageant world. It was what people liked best about her when she'd made that lemonade, and it was why the entire country rallied around her during her short-lived reign. She wasn't sure why she'd let Greg convince her that she needed to be a certain type of mother. Beauty queens and mothers came in all shapes and sizes. Melanie would find her way, just like she always had. And if she couldn't find one, she'd make one. She just hoped Cap still wanted to walk hand in hand with her while she did it.

The emotional roller coaster of the last few days had taken its toll, though, and Melanie fell asleep as the live feed from the pageant was winding down. She wasn't sure how long she'd been napping when she was awakened by a gentle kiss on her forehead.

"Wake up, Sleeping Beauty," Cap whispered, his breath warm on her cheek.

Melanie let her eyelashes flutter open, and there he was—sitting on the edge of her bed, tenderly brushing the hair from her eyes.

She grinned up at him. "You were an amazing pageant host. Bert Parks, eat your heart out."

Cap arched an eyebrow. "I'm covered in glitter, and at one point, Wade had to use a fire extinguisher on a flaming baton."

"Everyone looks good with a sparkle." She reached up to ruffle his hair and a puff of glitter fell out. "And who better to have around for a flaming-baton incident than the captain of the fire department? You did a better job than I ever could have."

He reached for her hand and brought it to his lips for a kiss. "How are you feeling?"

She nodded, tears blurring her vision. "Happy, especially now that you're here."

"I rushed back as soon as the festivities ended. Eli recruited the lacrosse team to help dismantle everything." Cap took a deep breath. "Mel, I'm not sure he can adequately express how sorry he is for what he did. I'm not trying to make excuses for him. I'm really not, but—"

She held up a hand to stop him. "Don't. We don't need to talk about it anymore. While I've been lying here, I've had some time to do some serious thinking."

Cap's lips twitched into a tentative smile. "Have you now? So what do you think?"

A tear slipped down her cheek, and Cap brushed it away with the pad of his thumb. Melanie really didn't want to cry right now, and not just because when she moved to Vermont she'd given up the beauty queen's best friend—waterproof mascara. She didn't want to become a blubbering mess until she'd made one thing perfectly clear. "I think I was wrong before. If today has taught me anything, it's that crowns and picket fences go together quite nicely."

Cap's face split into a wide grin. "Is that so?"

"Yes." Melanie nodded, crying in earnest. But at least she'd made it through what she needed to say first.

Mostly, anyway.

She sat up to kiss him through her tears, and when he wrapped his arms around her and held her close, she whispered into his warm, masculine neck. "I love you, Cap. And I want to be a family with you and Eli and my baby...*our* baby. Ask me again. Please?"

Cap pressed a kiss to her hair, and when he spoke, she could hear the smile on his lips. "Oh, darlin'. What perfect timing, because I brought you a little treat from the cupcake truck."

He leaned over and reached for a cupcake sitting on her nightstand. He must have placed it there before he'd woken her up. It smelled divine, like rich vanilla and—because they were in Lovestruck—a hint of pure Vermont sugar maple.

Then Melanie took a closer look at it, and she gasped. Her hand flew to her throat. The frosting was baby pink and sitting atop the perfect swirl of buttercream was a sparkling platinum engagement ring.

"Okay, I lied. I didn't actually come straight back from the pageant." Cap winked. "I made a quick stop at the jewelry store on Main. Eli helped me pick it out, and then he went back to folding chairs with his lacrosse friends."

"It's beautiful." Melanie's face hurt from smiling so hard. The ring was the most gorgeous, glittering thing she'd ever seen—her entire trophy case full of crowns included.

"So what do you say, sweetheart? Do you want to be my lemonade queen for as long as we both shall live?" Cap took the ring from atop the cupcake and slid it onto her finger. A perfect fit.

Melanie bit her lip. "On one teeny tiny condition."

Cap wove his fingertips through hers. The diamond on her hand glimmered like starlight. "What's that?"

"I'm going to need you to put my picket fence back up. Do you think you can handle it?"

"Can I handle it?" The corner of his mouth hitched into a lopsided grin. "As the most beautiful woman in the world once told me, I look like I know how to use a sledgehammer. So I think it can be arranged."

"Then it sounds like we have a deal." Melanie rose up to kiss him again, but paused just long enough to murmur against his lips. "My answer is yes. It always was and it always will be."

And that's how America's beloved lemon queen moved to tiny Lovestruck, Vermont, turned her lemons into lemonade and became the queen of Captain Jason McBride's heart.

* * * * *

For more great romances featuring heroine's looking to start fresh, try these other stories:

A New Foundation
By Rochelle Alers

She Dreamed of a Cowboy
By Joanna Sims

The Marine Makes Amends
By Victoria Pade

*Available now wherever
Harlequin Special Edition books
and ebooks are sold.*

COMING NEXT MONTH FROM

♦ HARLEQUIN

SPECIAL EDITION

#2833 BEFORE SUMMER ENDS
by Susan Mallery

Nissa Lang knows Desmond Stilling is out of her league. He's a CEO, she's a teacher. He's gorgeous, she's...not. So when her house-sitting gig falls through and Desmond offers her a place to stay for the summer, she vows not to reveal how she's felt about him since their first—and only—kiss.

#2834 THE LAST ONE HOME
The Bravos of Valentine Bay • by Christine Rimmer

Ian McNeill has returned to Valentine Bay to meet the biological family he can't remember. Along for the ride is his longtime best friend, single mom Ella Haralson. Will this unexpected reunion turn Ian into a family man in more ways than one?

#2835 AN OFFICER AND A FORTUNE
The Fortunes of Texas: The Hotel Fortune • by Nina Crespo

Captain Collin Waldon is on leave from the military, tending to his ailing father. He's not looking for romantic entanglements—*especially* not with Nicole Fortune, the executive chef of Roja Restaurant in the struggling Hotel Fortune. Yet these two unlikely lovers seem perfect for each other, until Collin's reassignment threatens their newfound bliss...

#2836 THE TWIN PROPOSAL
Lockharts Lost & Found • by Cathy Gillen Thacker

Mackenzie Lockhart just proposed to Griff Montgomery, her best bud since they were kids in foster care. Once Griff gets his well-deserved promotion, they can return to their independent lives. But when they cross the line from friends to lovers, there's no going back. With twins on the way, is this their chance to turn a temporary arrangement into a can't-lose formula for love?

#2837 THE MARINE'S BABY BLUES
The Camdens of Montana • by Victoria Pade

Tanner Camden never thought he'd end up getting a call that he might be a father—or that his ex had died, leaving little Poppy in the care of her sister, Addie Markham. Addie may have always resented him, but with their shared goal of caring for Poppy, they're willing to set aside their differences. Even if allowing their new feelings to bloom means both of them could get hurt when the paternity test results come back...

#2838 THE RANCHER'S FOREVER FAMILY
Texas Cowboys & K-9s • by Sasha Summers

Sergeant Hayden Mitchell's mission—give every canine veteran the perfect forever home. But when it comes to Sierra, a sweet Labrador, Hayden isn't sure Lizzie Vega fits the bill. When a storm leaves her stranded at his ranch, the hardened former military man wonders if Lizzie is the perfect match for Sierra...and him...

YOU CAN FIND MORE INFORMATION ON UPCOMING HARLEQUIN TITLES, FREE EXCERPTS AND MORE AT HARLEQUIN.COM.

HSECNM0421

"You're welcome to join me if you'd like. Unless you
have plans. It's Saturday, after all."

Plans as in a date? Yeah, not so much these days. In
fact, she hadn't been in a serious relationship since she
and James had broken up over two years ago.

"I don't date," she blurted before she could stop
herself. "I mean, I can, but I don't. Or I haven't been.
Um, lately."

She consciously pressed her lips together to stop
herself from babbling like an idiot, despite the fact that
the damage was done.

"So, dinner?" Desmond asked, rescuing her without
commenting on her babbling.

"I'd like that. After I shower. Meet back down here in half an hour?"

"Perfect."

There was an awkward moment when they both tried to go through the kitchen door at the same time. Desmond stepped back and waved her in front of him. She hurried out, then raced up the stairs and practically ran for her bedroom. Once there, she closed the door and leaned against it.

"Talking isn't hard," she whispered to herself. "You've been doing it since you were two. You know how to do this."

But when it came to being around Desmond, knowing and doing were two different things.

Don't miss
Before Summer Ends *by Susan Mallery,*
available May 2021 wherever
Harlequin Special Edition books and ebooks are sold.

Harlequin.com

Get 4 FREE REWARDS!

We'll send you 2 FREE Books plus <u>2 FREE Mystery Gifts.</u>

Harlequin Special Edition books relate to finding comfort and strength in the support of loved ones and enjoying the journey no matter what life throws your way.

FREE Value Over **$20**

YES! Please send me 2 FREE Harlequin Special Edition novels and my 2 FREE gifts (gifts are worth about $10 retail). After receiving them, if I don't wish to receive any more books, I can return the shipping statement marked "cancel." If I don't cancel, I will receive 6 brand-new novels every month and be billed just $4.99 per book in the U.S. or $5.74 per book in Canada. That's a savings of at least 12% off the cover price! It's quite a bargain! Shipping and handling is just 50¢ per book in the U.S. and $1.25 per book in Canada.* I understand that accepting the 2 free books and gifts places me under no obligation to buy anything. I can always return a shipment and cancel at any time. The free books and gifts are mine to keep no matter what I decide.

235/335 HDN GNMP

Name (please print)

Address _____ Apt. #

City _____ State/Province _____ Zip/Postal Code

Email: Please check this box ☐ if you would like to receive newsletters and promotional emails from Harlequin Enterprises ULC and its affiliates. You can unsubscribe anytime.

Mail to the **Harlequin Reader Service:**
IN U.S.A.: P.O. Box 1341, Buffalo, NY 14240-8531
IN CANADA: P.O. Box 603, Fort Erie, Ontario L2A 5X3

Want to try 2 free books from another series! Call 1-800-873-8635 or visit www.ReaderService.com.

*Terms and prices subject to change without notice. Prices do not include sales taxes, which will be charged (if applicable) based on your state or country of residence. Canadian residents will be charged applicable taxes. Offer not valid in Quebec. This offer is limited to one order per household. Books received may not be as shown. Not valid for current subscribers to Harlequin Special Edition books. All orders subject to approval. Credit or debit balances in a customer's account(s) may be offset by any other outstanding balance owed by or to the customer. Please allow 4 to 6 weeks for delivery. Offer available while quantities last.

Your Privacy—Your information is being collected by Harlequin Enterprises ULC, operating as Harlequin Reader Service. For a complete summary of the information we collect, how we use this information and to whom it is disclosed, please visit our privacy notice located at corporate.harlequin.com/privacy-notice. From time to time we may also exchange your personal information with reputable third parties. If you wish to opt out of this sharing of your personal information, please visit readerservice.com/consumerchoice or call 1-800-873-8635. **Notice to California Residents**—Under California law, you have specific rights to control and access your data. For more information on these rights and how to exercise them, visit corporate.harlequin.com/california-privacy.

HSE21R